Judah walked over to her and Darby couldn't yank her eyes from his.

He stopped in front of her, so close that she could feel his heat, see that he had a tiny scar on the corner of his left eye. His fingers gripped her hips and a tremor skittered through her. If she lifted herself onto her toes, just a little, her mouth would be aligned with his, and she would know his taste.

Don't do it, Darby. Bad, bad, dreadful idea.

Judah's other hand snaked around her back, splaying across the top of her butt as he gently pulled her toward him. Her breasts scraped his chest, her nipples puckering against the lace of her bra. She wanted his mouth there, she realized, shocked.

Darby ignored her brain's loud suggestion to leave and kept her eyes locked on his, seeing images of what could be in his eyes.

* * *

The Rival's Heir is part of
Harlequin Desire's #1 bestselling series,
Billionaires and Babies: Powerful men...wrapped
around their babies' little fingers.

Dear Reader,

In addition to being a Billionaires and Babies novel, this is the third book in my Love in Boston series.

Darby Brogan has always wanted a child. Now, rapidly approaching thirty, she is single and is informed that the best chance of her conceiving is within the next four to six months through IVF. Faced with this decision, Darby—a driven and independent architect and partner in a design firm with her twin and best friend—starts questioning whether her wish for a child is rooted in her inability to fail.

Judah Huntley is one of the world's most exciting architects and is back in Boston to bid on a commission to design a new art museum. After finding his girlfriend, opera-singing sensation and heiress, in bed with his younger brother, he has no use for relationships. Having been his brother's primary caregiver until he left for college, Judah is also determined never to have children. He's been an almost father, it wasn't fun and, because his brother grew up with addiction issues, Judah believes he isn't cut out to be a parent.

So what happens when a baby girl, very unexpectedly, falls into their lives?

Happy reading,

Joss

Connect with me at www.josswoodbooks.com.

Twitter: @JossWoodBooks

Facebook: Joss Wood Author

JOSS WOOD

THE RIVAL'S HEIR

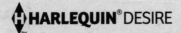

Recycling programs
for this product may
not exist in your area.

ISBN-13: 978-1-335-97190-6

The Rival's Heir

Copyright © 2018 by Joss Wood

Printed in U.S.A.

HARLEQUIN®
™www.Harlequin.com

Joss Wood loves books and traveling—especially to the wild places of Southern Africa and, well, anywhere. She's a wife, a mom to two teenagers and slave to two cats. After a career in local economic development, she now writes full-time. Joss is a member of Romance Writers of America and Romance Writers of South Africa.

Books by Joss Wood

Harlequin Desire

The Ballantyne Billionaires

His Ex's Well-Kept Secret
One Night to Forever
The CEO's Nanny Affair
Little Secrets: Unexpectedly Pregnant

Love in Boston

Friendship on Fire
Hot Christmas Kisses
The Rival's Heir

Visit her Author Profile page at Harlequin.com, or josswoodbooks.com, for more titles.

This book is dedicated to anyone
who has struggled with infertility.
I get how hard it is.
You have my love and prayers.

Prologue

Callie Brogan looked around the lavish crowded function room at the Lockwood Country Club and edged her way to the side. She'd attended, and hosted, many parties in this very room and knew all the escape routes.

A few steps backward and her back was against the floor-to-ceiling glass doors. She fiddled behind her and yep, there was the handle. Callie pushed it down, felt the door swing open and as quickly as she could, ducked onto the small balcony that ran the length of the ballroom. She closed the door behind her, allowing her eyes to adjust to the darkness.

She didn't mind the dark, nor the cold—in fact she welcomed both. Anything was better than loud music, louder laughter and incessant chatter. Staring a new year in the face, she needed a few minutes of quiet, just to think.

Her beloved husband, Ray, was gone. He had been for many years.

It was time to let him go.

She couldn't hold on to him while she had an affair with the man she'd come here with tonight. It wasn't fair to either of them.

Callie looked down at the ring Ray had put on her finger over thirty years ago. She turned it around and around again. It was time to take it off, to put it away or at the very least, move it to her right hand. She wasn't Ray's anymore.

And while she might be sleeping with Mason—adventurous, inked and hot—she didn't belong to him either. She needed a new life, one that was hers alone. She wanted more. She no longer wanted to be the person she was, but she also didn't know who she wanted to be.

She had to reinvent herself.

But how?

Before she could finish the thought, a soft coat settled on her shoulders, broad hands on her hips.

"Are you okay?" Mason asked, his warm breath on her ear.

"Fine," Callie answered, wincing at her terse answer. She'd just wanted five minutes on her own, to figure things out.

But it was New Year's Eve, they were at a ball, and she had tomorrow to think about her life and why she was so discontented, in spite of having a fantastically sexy man sharing her sheets. The music was playing, the countdown would soon start and her issues could wait.

Callie looped her arms around Mason's neck, pushing a smile onto her face.

"Let's go inside, grab a drink and dance," Callie said, trying for gaiety.

Mason stepped back and shook his head. "I've been watching you for the last ten minutes. I saw you playing with your ring."

Callie frowned down at her hand and the big diamond winked back at her. "Okay?" she replied, confused.

Mason pinched the bridge of his nose. "Just once, Callie, I'd like to go somewhere, do something, that isn't tinged with the memories of your husband."

Before Callie could tell him that she hadn't been thinking about Ray, he continued, "Is it going to be like this for the next year, two years, ten? I'm asking so I know how long I'll be competing for your attention."

Callie felt the burn of shock, the heat of anger. "That's not fair."

"No, what's not fair is you mentally wandering off to join him while I am here. What's not fair is you wearing his ring while I bring you to orgasm, his picture facedown in the drawer next to your bed. Do you bring him out when we're done, Callie? Sneak him back into place when I leave?"

She did. God. And Mason knew.

Callie lifted her hands in protest. Because she felt embarrassed, she went on the attack. "Why are you hassling me? I thought this was just an affair. Why are you sounding all possessive and jealous?"

Mason opened his mouth to respond, then cursed before snapping it shut. His expression cooled, then turned inscrutable. "You're right. Forgive me." His deep voice was coated with frost.

From inside, the revelers started to count down to the New Year and when the crowd roared, Mason bent down and kissed her cheek, as remote as an Antarctic iceberg. "Happy New Year, Callie."

When Callie went back inside just a few minutes later, Mason was gone.

One

Darby Brogan listened with half an ear to the presentation but couldn't make herself concentrate. Unlike the other architects in the room who were listening intently, her thoughts were a million miles away from the project of a lifetime. Designing Boston's newest art museum was, suddenly and unexpectedly, the very last thing on her mind.

Darby crossed her legs, tapped her phone against her knee and mentally urged the speaker to hurry up. Modern, fresh, distinctive, ecologically friendly… Yes, she got it. This was all in the bid documents.

Her phone vibrated in her hand. Darby swiped her thumb across the screen and quickly read the messages posted in the group only she, her twin, Jules, and their best friend and business partner, DJ, had access to.

Where are you? Why aren't you back? How did your appointment with Dr. Mackenzie go?

Darby typed a quick reply to DJ's question.

At the museum bid presentation. Should be back in an hour or so.

Darby saw that Jules was typing and waited for her message to pop up on the screen. As she expected, it had nothing to do with work and everything to do with the appointment Darby had just come from.

Tell us!

Darby wished she hadn't recently pushed DJ to be more open and forthcoming. It made it difficult for Darby to keep her own secrets from her best friend and her twin.

It's not good. Basically, I'm running out of time. If I want a child, I should attempt IVF in the next six months.

She waited a beat before adding:

So that's a big decision I need to make. And quickly.

Judging by their lack of an immediate response, Darby knew her friends were absorbing her news, trying, like she was, to make sense of what she'd learned.

Darby wanted children. Being a mommy was her biggest wish. But despite knowing that she was going to have problems carrying a child, she'd always believed she'd need to face her infertility issues sometime in the future. She'd thought she had time, options, but…no. Her condition had been upgraded from serious to severe and she'd been told to expect a hysterectomy within the next few years.

And she had yet to hit thirty.

I thought I'd have a husband, at least a partner, when I needed to go there. I never imagined I'd have to do this—if I'm going to do this—alone.

You'll never be alone!!!

What Jules said, DJ added.

They were great, and she loved them, but Darby imagined strong arms, a broad chest, a male perspective. She'd been called beautiful, strong and smart, but she still went to bed alone every night.

Being an alpha female was hard enough for most men to accept. Being an alpha female with infertility issues seemed a step too far. The reality was that she couldn't afford to wait any longer to find a man who shared her dreams for a family; she had no more time to waste. If she wanted a child, she'd be doing it now, solo, albeit with the help of science. And a sperm donor.

DJ's name popped up again on her screen.

How can we help?

Darby smiled, so glad these women were in her life. Darby ignored her burning eyes and straightened her shoulders. It was bad news, sure, but she hadn't received a death sentence. Her dreams were in ICU, but she wasn't.

Keep it in perspective, Brogan. Humor, as she'd learned, was always a good deterrent to negativity, so she thought a moment before typing again.

I'll expect you to help me select a sperm donor.

Any excuse to openly ogle guys! Jules's answer flashed on her screen. I'm there.

DJ repeated the sentiment, adding a couple of heart-eyed emoji to convey her excitement. Darby knew they were just being kind. They were both engaged to and head over heels in love with smart, successful, stupidly sexy men.

Darby was not jealous...

Well, maybe a little.

They all—including her mother!—had hot guys in their beds. Jules was engaged to her childhood friend; DJ and her long-term on-again, off-again lover had recently decided to be permanently on. As for Darby's mother, Callie? She was having an affair with a scorching hot man a decade younger.

Darby wouldn't mind a sexy tattooed man to have

some fun with. Her life for the past year or so had been all work and very little play… Actually, that pretty much summed up her life in total. She didn't play much at all, she never had.

After a lifetime of school and college success, she'd recently been named one of the most exciting 40 Architects Under 40 in the latest edition of a well-known design publication. She was a partner in what was described as the most successful design house in Boston, possibly on all the East Coast. She was reasonably attractive, wealthy and healthy. Well, except for her annoying reproductive system.

And she was single…

So very, very single.

She felt panic tickle her throat. What if she were incapable of loving someone, of being in a have-it-all partnership? What if she was too independent, too strong willed, too competitive to build her life with a man?

As for a solo attempt at motherhood…could she do this?

Darby shifted in her seat. She refused to give negative thoughts space in her brain. She wanted a child and she could be a single mom. It was okay that she'd yet to meet her special someone. She was glad she hadn't wasted her valuable time on a he'll-do guy.

If she was going to settle down, she wanted someone who wanted what she did…everything. Kids, a kick-ass career, a stable, respectful relationship.

World peace, an end to famine…

Darby frowned when she realized that the organization's director was no longer speaking. She looked around the ballroom, seeing that the attendees had shifted their focus to the back of the room. Turning in her seat, her brows lifted when she saw the lone figure leaning against the wall, one ankle crossed over the other.

Oh…

Oh…*wow.*

Judah Huntley was better looking in person than the pictures she'd seen of him online. Taller, too. Being tall herself, she guesstimated he was six-two or six-three, and under his charcoal, obviously designer Italian suit, his body was tougher, harder, more muscular than she would have expected. Broad chest, long legs, thick arms and a masculine face. Stubble covered his cheeks and jaw, his nose looked like it had been broken once, maybe twice and his thick wavy espresso-colored hair looked like he routinely combed it with his fingers.

Sexy, built and the brightest architectural mind of his generation.

Darby swallowed, conscious that her mouth was dry and her heart was banging against her chest. There was an unfamiliar heat between her legs— welcome back, libido! Damn, she wouldn't mind taking Judah Huntley out for a spin.

Whoa, Brogan, not like you.

The men she dated and—very rarely—slept with had to work damn hard to get her to that point but

Darby knew Judah Huntley would just have to crook his finger and she'd come running.

Maybe it was her kooky state of mind, yet here she was, panting over a man across the room.

Darby couldn't pull her eyes from Huntley's fallen-angel face. *Be sensible, Brogan.* This scorched-earth attraction was an aberration, nothing to be concerned about. She was only intrigued by Judah Huntley because he was such a phenomenal architect, because he'd designed that ecohouse in Denmark that was a brilliant piece of art, as was that ski lodge in Davos and the new headquarters for one of the world's leading software companies in Austin. He was creative and innovative, throwing together contrasting materials and techniques and making them work.

And he was sexy enough to make her soul ache.

Dark eyes—black? blue?—under strong brows met hers.

And Darby felt the world shift beneath her.

A small smile pulled the corners of his mouth upward and she placed her hand to her heart. God, the way he looked at her, like he was imagining her naked…

He straightened, pushed his hands into the pockets of his suit pants and she saw that his stomach was flat. She remembered a photo of him running on a beach in Cyprus… That muscled, ridged stomach. Just looking at him was more pleasure than she'd had in a while.

Unbidden, the image of her eggs and his sperm

colliding in a petri dish, creating a baby in the lab, jumped into her head. If she imagined them in bed together, practicing the art of making babies the old-fashioned way, her panties might explode.

Darby fought the temptation to get up, walk over to him, hold out her hand and lead him away. She didn't think he'd say no. Damn, she was tempted.

"Miss Brogan? *Miss! Brogan!*"

Darby turned her head at the irritated voice of the director at the front of the room. What was his problem? Frowning, she looked around and saw the amused faces of her colleagues.

"May I continue?"

Darby quickly nodded, her face flaming. She heard the muffled snickers. Dammit, the entire room had caught her looking at Judah Huntley. Since, as her family frequently told her, she had the most expressive face in the history of the world, they all knew she'd been imagining Huntley naked.

Darby slid down in her seat, only just resisting the urge to cover her face with her hands. Even if she found the guts to proposition him—a very big *if*—sleeping with Judah Huntley wasn't an option. Especially since she was now embarrassed beyond all belief.

Darby kept her eyes on the speaker while she fought the urge to look back and take just one more peek. *Yeah, good plan, just embarrass yourself further, Brogan, add some fuel to the fire.*

It took all her willpower to keep her eyes forward

and when the presentation finally ended—the longest ten minutes in the world—Darby stood up and oh-so casually looked across the room.

Judah Huntley was gone.

Six weeks later

Judah Huntley took a sip of overly sweet champagne from the glass in his hand and tried not to wince. God, he hated these functions. He strongly believed in the power of an old-fashioned email, quietly stating whether he'd been awarded the commission or not. Putting on a suit and noose and making small talk was his level of hell.

But Jonathan, his business manager, had RSVP'd on Judah's behalf, saying that he'd be glad to attend the foundation's cocktail party. He'd also promised that if Huntley and Associates was commissioned to design the new art museum, Judah would hire a local architect to be the firm's local liaison.

It made sense to hire someone local to do the grunt work of visiting the planning offices, research, smoothing the way. The Boston-based architect wouldn't do any drafting or design work; Judah had an experienced team back in New York to implement his ideas. They were the best and brightest of the bunch and routinely met his high standards.

As a winner of two of the world's most prestigious architecture awards, Judah knew his interest in designing the art museum was unexpected.

It wasn't a big project or even a lucrative one. Since the project was being funded by a nonprofit, his design fees would be laughable. But thanks to international businessmen with very deep pockets who wanted his name attached to their buildings, Judah had a fat bank account and could afford to take on a project at cost.

He had buildings all over the world but had yet to design one in Boston, his hometown. He wanted to create something that was beautiful and functional, something Bostonians would enjoy. He was renowned for his innovative corporate buildings and envelope-pushing mansions but there was something special, something intoxicating, about designing a building to hold art and treasures. The box had to be as exciting, as electrifying as the contents…

And that was why he was standing in a stuffy ballroom waiting for someone to announce what everyone already knew: Judah would be awarded the project.

Upsides to being in Boston were a gorgeous site and an interesting project. Downside? Being in Boston. The smells, the air, the buildings all made him remember how his life used to be. Stifling. Demanding. Claustrophobic. Long on responsibility and short on fun.

Judah was grateful for the feminine hand on his arm that jerked him back to the present. An attractive woman stood in front of him, blond hair, red lips, bold eyes. He chatted with her politely, but she wasn't the woman who'd first come to mind.

The last time he'd stood in this room, he'd locked eyes with a younger, sexier blonde who'd made his stomach bungee jump. Initially, she'd reminded him of a storybook Cinderella, all flashing eyes and tiny frame, but then he'd caught the look in her eyes, on her face, and decided that she was more a duchess than a princess, more sophisticated than simple.

He wondered if she was here again tonight.

But, if she was, what did it matter? Though he'd been rocked by their instinctual attraction—when last had he felt such an instant physical reaction to anyone?—the thought of making small talk, doing the dating dance, felt like too much effort.

Chatting up a woman, taking her back to his hotel room and having sex was the mental equivalent of riding an immensely popular roller coaster. Patience was required to get on the ride, there was the brief sensation of pleasure, then the inevitable anticlimax when the cart rolled to a stop.

After Carla, he'd ridden as many roller coasters as he could. A year and too many women later, he'd realized that mindless sex with mindless women wasn't working for him and he went cold turkey. In the past eighteen months, he'd gone from being monogamous to being a player to being a monk.

Judah sighed. While no guy rapidly approaching his forties preferred having solo sex, he did like having a life that was drama-free.

But that blonde he'd seen here before—tall, slim, stunningly sexy—was the first woman in six months who'd caught his interest. She'd made his core temperature rise. She had the face of a naughty pixie, the body of a lingerie model and the eyes of a water nymph. When he'd looked at her, reality faded. All he could see was her, stretched out on a rug in front of a roaring fire, naked on the white sands of Tahiti or on the cool marble of a designer kitchen. Hell, up against the fabric-covered wall of an intensely uninteresting hotel ballroom.

He'd wanted her.

And because he'd been so damned tempted to walk over, take her hand and find the closest private space where he could put his hands on that body, he'd acted like the adult he professed to be and left. He didn't want mindless sex anymore, but the thought of anything more—becoming emotionally involved, making a connection—terrified him.

So he was in no-man's-land, dating himself. And, man, was he so tired of that...

Half concentrating on the conversation with the woman in front of him, Judah looked up to see the director of the foundation heading to the podium. Standing at the back of the room, Judah's height allowed him to see over the heads of most of the guests and he recognized some candidates from the meeting weeks ago.

He cursed himself when he realized he was looking for a bright blond head and exceptional legs.

"Ladies and gentlemen, on behalf of the Grantham-Ford Foundation…"

Judah pushed his hands into the pockets of his suit pants, tuned out the opening remarks of the chairman of the board and looked toward the door, his attention caught by an elder man in a suit, his tanned face scanning the crowd, obviously looking for someone. He looked vaguely familiar, like a worried version of someone from Judah's past.

Intrigued, Judah edged his way closer to the door. The man's dark eyes caught his movement and Judah saw relief cross his face. The man was looking for *him*. But why here at this hotel, in the middle of a function? Judah had an office, an assistant who managed his schedule.

Odd.

"We were all blown away by the designs submitted and it was difficult to make a choice…"

Judah ignored the droning voice and frowned as the man eased away from the doorway, gesturing for Judah to join him in the hallway. Judah tossed a look over his shoulder, guessing the director would ramble on for a few more minutes—the man seemed to like the sound of his own voice. Judah pulled the door to the room partially closed behind him. If he was needed, he had no doubt someone would find him.

"Mr. Huntley! I am so glad I managed to track you down."

Judah's heart sank when he heard the masculine version of Carla's heavy Italian accent. Judah scowled. His ex, the opera-singing heiress, had hit a new low if she was sending her minions to deliver her messages. Judah had nothing to say to her face or via her employees. She'd cheated on him—he was pretty sure it hadn't been the first time—but he'd caught her. She and her lover had been in *his* bed, in *his* apartment. Naked on his sheets.

Judah didn't share, ever. Infidelity was his hard limit. And he was still pissed that he'd felt compelled to buy a new bed and give those expensive sheets to a charity shop. He'd thought about selling his apartment, but that was going a step too far. Carla wasn't worth the sacrifice of his stunning views of Central Park.

Judah held up his hand. "Not interested."

"Wait, Mr. Huntley."

Judah lifted an eyebrow dismissively. "You have thirty seconds and I'm only giving you that much because this evening is sadly lacking in entertainment."

Thin shoulders pushed back and an elegant hand smoothed a lock of silver hair off the man's forehead. "I am Maximo Rossi. I am Carla's personal lawyer."

Okay. And what did Carla's personal lawyer want from Judah? Thanks to being the sole beneficiary of her father's billions, Carla had more money than God, along with her luscious body and stunning face. She also had the voice of an angel. They hadn't had any contact for months, so why now? Judah felt his stomach twist itself into a Gordian knot. This couldn't be good.

He forced himself to remain calm. "Is Carla okay?"

"She's fine…mostly."

Oh, God. He recognized the weariness in the older man's eyes, the frustration that dealing with Carla Barlos incurred. The man probably had a stomach ulcer and high blood pressure. Judah could sympathize. Carla was hard work.

"What does that mean?" Judah demanded, hearing the apprehension in Rossi's voice.

"Bertolli has written a new opera, one just for her."

Bertolli's music sounded like screeching cats, but what did Judah know? But even he, philistine that he was, understood how a big a deal it was to have Bertolli, the most exciting composer in the world, build an opera around Carla.

"It's a morality tale. Carla's lead character is a crusader for moral reform."

While Judah appreciated the irony, he didn't understand why Rossi was here, telling him this. Why should Judah care what Carla was up to? He hadn't seen her for more than eighteen months.

Deciding he was done here, Judah was about to excuse himself when he heard the arrival of the elevator. The doors opened and a long leg, ending in a blush-colored pump, emerged from the box. A frothy peppermint-colored dress danced around slim thighs.

She was here, she was back.

Rossi forgotten, Judah's eyes wandered upward,

taking in a thin belt around a tiny waist, skating up a narrow chest. Her breasts were fantastic, small but perky. Athletic but not overly so, fit but still oh-so feminine. And God, that face.

Judah felt his cold heart sputter as blood drained south. A wide mouth made for kissing, high cheekbones, eyes the color of zinc under arched brows. Blond hair pulled back into a sleek ponytail.

He'd last seen her across a crowded room weeks ago. He'd thought her sexy then. Now, he upgraded that assessment to heart-stoppingly hot.

He wanted her. Now, immediately, up against that wall, his hands on those tanned thighs, his tongue on her neck, her nipple, her naval. He could go back to being a monk tomorrow...

But she had yet to notice him. Her attention was taken by the other occupants of the elevator, a black-haired, dark-eyed baby held by a hard-faced, middle-aged woman. The woman held the kid like she would hold a test tube of poison, awkward and fearful. He didn't blame her; he wasn't a kid person either.

He used to be, but that was a long time ago. When he was young and stupid.

Rossi cleared his throat. "That is my assistant and the baby is Jacquetta Huntley. Carla needs you to take her for at least six months. She can't be responsible for her and prepare for the biggest performance of her career."

While Judah struggled to make sense of the man's

words, a booming voice from the front of the room rolled into the hallway.

"I am pleased and proud to announce that the architect designing the Grantham-Ford Art Museum will be Judah Huntley. Judah, please come forward and say a few words."

Judah's eyes darted between three faces: Rossi, the baby and the blonde.

It was official. He'd just fallen down Alice's rabbit hole.

Two

Three things occurred to Darby at the same time.

One, Judah Huntley was more gorgeous than she remembered.

Two, he had a kid he didn't know about.

Three, hers wasn't the only messed-up life.

Oh, he was good. On hearing he had a child, his expression barely changed, but his ink-blue eyes held disbelief and a heavy dose of *WTF*. The baby, stunningly gorgeous with rosy cheeks and hair the color of bitter chocolate, looked at them from the stiff arms of the woman carrying her.

Darby knew she should move away, she should give them some privacy but...

She wasn't that noble, and this was too good to miss. How would Judah Huntley juggle the announcement of the commission *and* the news that he had a child? Would he flip, freeze, flee?

Darby couldn't wait to find out.

The baby let out a soft cry, Judah was called to the front of the room again and the weary woman took a step toward Judah, holding the baby out like a parcel. Judah threw up his hands in a hell-no gesture and the baby responded by letting out a shriller cry.

Darby forgot about the drama playing out in front of her eyes and focused on that small face scrunched up and turning red. The wails grew louder and someone she recognized as one of the foundation's board members appeared at the door.

"Mr. Huntley, they are calling for you. You've been awarded the design contract."

No surprise there. Judah was an amazing architect.

But his ability to ignore a screaming baby annoyed her. Pushing past the lawyer, she reached for the little girl, ignoring the look of relief on the older woman's face. Tucking the baby into the crook of her arm, Darby placed her pinkie finger in the little girl's mouth and felt the tug of tiny lips.

Darby looked at Judah. "She's hungry."

He threw his hands up in the air and shook his head. "Not my problem."

"Apparently it is," Darby responded tartly.

"Um… Mr. Huntley. Really, you need to come back inside." The man tugged the sleeve of Judah's jacket.

Darby noticed, *again*, that the jacket covered a set of rather big arms and broad shoulders. Judah's easy dismissal of this beautiful baby was irritating, but her hormones had yet to receive the message that she shouldn't be imagining what Huntley's body looked like under that expensive suit.

Judah pushed his hand through his thick, expertly cut hair and she heard the barely audible swear he dropped. Yeah, Huntley wasn't having a good day.

He gripped the bridge of his nose. After a brief pause, he lifted his head and Darby saw the determination on his face, the assertiveness in his eyes. There was something superhot about an alpha male doing his thing...

Judah nodded to the closed door of the ballroom.

"I'm going to go back in there to accept this damn commission. Rossi, you are going to take the baby with you and you will call me and we will arrange a suitable time to meet and discuss Carla's insanity. Do not ambush me again." That dark blue gaze scraped over her and he shook his head. "You, I have no idea who you are but if you'd kindly give the kid back, we can all go on with our lives."

His tone suggested that he wasn't interested in hearing any arguments and when no one spoke, he turned around and walked back into the ballroom, the board member following closely behind. Darby heard the audience's roar of applause and looked down at the little girl in her arms.

She had Judah's nose and the shape of his eyes and

Darby could see the hint of Judah's shallow dimple in the baby's left cheek. Like his, the baby's hair was dark, her sweet brows strong. She was utterly perfect and those deep dark eyes—brown, not blue—looked up at Darby's, content to suckle on her pinkie.

She was, possibly, the most beautiful baby Darby had ever seen and as she'd been obsessed by babies for longer than was healthy, she'd seen more than a lot. This little girl looked like what she was, the offspring of two boundlessly beautiful people.

Before his death, Darby's father had been a well-known Boston businessman and her parents had been, at one time, the heart of Boston society, so she'd had a taste of fame. But Huntley and his ex-girlfriend were famous on an entirely different level. Carla, an exciting, lushly beautiful, stunningly wealthy opera-singing heiress, had millions of social media followers and was tabloid gold. Thanks to his talent, his stupidly sexy body, and his penchant for dating models and actresses, Judah was also a media golden boy.

They might be famous, but Darby wasn't impressed by either of the little girl's parents right now.

How could Carla just shove her child out of her life, pass her on like she was an unwanted package? And why hadn't Judah stepped up? Didn't they realize that a child was a gift, indescribably precious? What was wrong with these people?

Had the world gone mad?

The baby burped and then her face scrunched up,

her eyes closing. Darby had enough experience to know that the little girl was about to fill her diaper. The telltale smell wafted up and Darby half smiled. Yep, there it was.

Darby looked up and saw the two lawyers grimace in immediate expressions of distaste.

"She needs changing," Darby stated just in case they hadn't made the connection between the smell and the problem.

Identical looks of horror and two steps back. "No! No, no, no!"

The baby squirmed in Darby's arms and let out a wail loud enough to be heard in Fenway Park. Okay, time to go.

The baby was stunningly cute and too adorable for words, but Darby had come here to work. It wasn't a surprise that Huntley had been awarded the project, but Darby knew there were lots of well-heeled socialites in that room with money to burn. Some of them might want a summer place designed or a house renovated.

Business had been a bit slow lately and she needed a new, lucrative project. She also needed to finish the renovations to two small apartment buildings she owned in Back Bay and get them on the market, but she knew it might take some time to sell them at the price she wanted.

Thank God she was due her quarterly dividend check from Winston and Brogan tomorrow; that was the money she'd allocated to her IVF fund. With that money and any she managed to save over the next four months, she could have the procedure in five months' time. At the thought, her stomach churned, then burned.

Unlike Huntley and his ex, she wanted a child.

Didn't she?

The two Europeans exchanged a long look as if they were silently arguing about who was going to do the honors of changing the little girl. They both looked horrified.

"I need to get going," Darby said.

A charming smile crossed the lawyer's face. "The nanny we hired to look after Jacquetta since we left Italy has been dismissed. Could you change her since neither of us knows how?"

"What makes you think I do?" Darby asked.

Mr. Slick just shrugged, and Darby knew she was being played. It had been years since she'd changed a diaper, but she'd looked after babies as a teenager. She was sure it was like riding a bike; one didn't just forget. And God, if she left little Jacquetta—goodness, what a mouthful—in their hands, the kid would be more miserable than she was now. It was one diaper, Darby could deal.

Darby held out her hand for the bag draped over the lady's shoulder. Darby would change Jacquetta—*Jac*—make up a bottle for the little girl and send them on their way. There was no doubt she'd remember this encounter for the rest of her life: hot guy, cute kid, drama…

"There's a baby room just around the corner." Darby jerked her head at the woman. "You're coming with me."

"Perché?"

Why? Jeez, these people were seriously whacked. "Because you don't just hand over a baby to a stranger, that's why."

Mr. Slick smiled at her. "The corridor ends just beyond the restroom so there is nowhere to take little Jacquetta. If you wanted to steal her, you'd have to pass by us. And we'll be here waiting."

Darby frowned, unease crawling across her skin.

"Besides, this is one of the best hotels in Boston, there are cameras everywhere." Mr. Slick winced as Jacquetta's cries escalated in volume.

Dammit. She was going to do this.

Darby started to walk down the hallway. Feeling eyes on her, she looked back. Her gut was screaming at her that their expressions were too bland, that she was being played. How the hell had she ended up in this situation?

Then Jac released a high-pitched scream and Darby looked down, her heart hurting over the little girl's distress. The baby, defenseless and innocent, had to come first. Darby would change her and make up a bottle, maybe give her a little cuddle and then Darby would hand her back.

Her life would go back to normal in ten minutes.

Darby walked down the corridor, her hand tapping Jac's little bottom, unable to resist dropping a kiss on the baby's curly head. In the baby changing room, Darby laid Jac on the soft changing table and looked down into the little girl's exquisite face.

"Should I have one just like you?"

Jac, being no more than nine months old, didn't have a clue.

Little Jac sucked her bottle as Darby walked back down the hallway, her shoulders aching from the un-accustomed weight of holding a baby and a seriously heavy baby bag. The baby was clean and happy, and Darby could hand her over and go back to her life.

Except that, when she turned the corner, there was nobody to hand the baby back to.

Hearing noise from the elevator, Darby spun around and saw the two lawyers standing in the elevator.

"Give the baby to Judah Huntley," Mr. Slick told her, his words sliding between the closing doors.

Darby couldn't believe what they'd done. They'd left Jac with a stranger! How did they know she wasn't a psycho, that she wouldn't just walk off with the baby?

Dumping the heavy bag into the stroller and leaving it in the hallway, Darby pushed open the door to the ballroom with her hip and scanned the audience. It wasn't difficult to find Huntley since he was taller than pretty much everyone. His dark head was bent to better hear the words of an olive-skinned bru-nette wearing a low top. Her expression brazenly suggested that she wouldn't say no if Huntley invited her to take a tour of his guest suite, or the nearest closet.

Irrationally annoyed, Darby focused on the photographs flashing onto the presentation screen on the far side of the room, each image stealing her breath. The first photo was of Huntley's proposed design for the Grantham-Ford museum and it was fantastic. The building looked curvy and feminine, sultry and almost, dare she say it, sexy. It was stunning and, dammit, so much better than her own design. The man deserved to win the commission. As images of his previous designs rolled across the wall, she stood there, blown away yet again by his talent.

Darby pulled her gaze away from the images and looked back to the creator of those magnificent buildings, surprised to find his eyes on her. God, he was a good-looking man. An intriguing combination of sexy and smart, tough and taciturn.

She jerked her head to summon him over and studied him as he made his way toward her, graceful despite his height and large frame.

Stepping back into the hall, Darby glanced down at the sleeping bundle in her arms, smiling at the very feminine version of that masculine man heading her way. She'd hand Jac over to her him and remind herself that this beautiful child was not her problem. She had her own baby issues to figure out.

As Judah reached the door, the chairman of the

board, so in love with his own voice, tapped his glass with a spoon and the room fell quiet.

Puffed up with self-importance, he spoke into the microphone. "Given this foundation's commitment to supporting Bostonian talent, I understand that some of our local professionals might be upset that the design has been awarded to a New York–based architect, but the winning design was simply outstanding. That said, it is my great pleasure to announce that Huntley and Associates is looking for a local architect to work with Judah Huntley on the art museum project."

The room erupted into clapping and cheers, and Darby looked at Judah, her eyebrows raised.

Judah shrugged before murmuring, "He's making it sound like more than it is. My new hire will be little more than a glorified intern, the liaison between the foundation and myself."

Darby felt the sharp nip of annoyance. "She or he won't get to work on the construction documentation?"

"I have a team back in New York for that. They are a well-oiled machine."

So the position was not something she was interested in. She was an architect, not an intern. "Do you intend to pay this person or are they expected to work for the honor of being able to put your name as a reference on their resume?"

He didn't react to her snippiness. "They'll be paid."

"How much?" Darby demanded. She wasn't interested in working as an intern but she was curious what world-renowned architects paid.

Judah named a figure and Darby's mouth fell open. That much? Seriously? Well, wow. At that rate, her interest rose. Pity he was a baby-rejecting jerk or she'd put her name in the hat.

Jac hiccuped in her sleep and Judah's eyes shifted to the living doll in Darby's arms. She looked into his face for any hint of acceptance or compassion and felt disappointed when she found none. She didn't like him, but she reluctantly conceded that his hard and brooding expression was as sexy as his debonair and urbane facade. The many faces of Judah Huntley, Darby mused.

This man, who is uninterested in his own child, is the opposite of what you are looking for in a man.

"Why do you still have the child?"

Darby narrowed her eyes at his clipped tone. "I have her because I changed her diaper for your friends. They said they'd be waiting for me in the hallway, but they left before I could hand her back."

Judah glared at her and in the dim light, she saw concern jump into his eyes. "What?"

He was a smart guy, why was this difficult to understand? "Do try to keep up, Huntley. I changed her diaper, made up some formula and when I got back, the two Italians were in the elevator. I thought about chasing them down, then figured the easier option was to hand Jac over to you."

"Jack? Her name is Jack?"

Darby heard the weird note in his voice and wondered why the name rocked his boat. "They called her Jacquetta but that's too much of a mouthful, so I shortened it to Jac," Darby replied. "Here you go."

Darby tried to hand Judah the child, but he stepped back, looking horrified.

Oh, no! She'd already done more than enough. "This is a child, Huntley! *Your* child, apparently. You don't just get to throw your hands up in the air and step back. She's a baby, not a package you can refuse."

Judah rubbed the back of his neck. "Damned Carla. What the hell is she playing at?"

"So, I take it Jac is a bit of a surprise? That you didn't know about her?"

"Of course I didn't know about her! She's not—" Judah snapped his mouth shut and gripped the bridge of his nose in frustration.

That he'd been about to say that the baby wasn't his was easy to work out. But Darby wasn't that much of an idiot. Judah might not want Jac to be his, but the little girl was a carbon copy of him, down to her nose and stubborn chin.

Judah glanced down at Jac and lifted his big shoulders. "I can't take her."

Oh, God, she was so done with this. Darby lifted her free hand, gripped Judah's lapel and stood up on her toes, annoyed to realize that she still needed more height to look him in the eye. "Listen to me, you spoiled, inconsiderate ass! This baby was brought to you by those useless fools and if I track them down, I will carve them up for leaving her with a stranger and then disappearing. I could've been a baby trafficker, a nut case, a psycho!"

Amusement jumped into Judah's eyes. "Are you?"

God, when he half smiled, that dimple deepened and her stomach quivered. It was like he just dialed his sexy factor up to lethal and—

Why was she thinking about that? She was supposed to be tearing him a new one! Sexy or not, he was going to get a very big piece of her mind. "You're an idiot if you can't see how much Jac looks like you! And even though I am the only one who seems to give a damn about this child, she is not my responsibility."

"You agreed to change her, you let them go. You could've handed her back."

Could he really be that unfeeling, that cold? This man who created art in buildings with such verve, such emotion in every line. How could he be so devoid of warmth?

"You heartless bastard! Do you know how lucky you are to have a child? Do you know how many people would love to be you?" Darby winced when her voice rose. Then she decided that she didn't care. Somebody needed to stand up for Jac, to put her first, and it seemed Darby had been nominated. "She's the innocent party and if you can't see that, then you are a complete and utter waste of space."

Darby knew she was panting, knew she was on the edge of tears and knew she had to leave before she lost it. She also had to leave before she walked away with the baby nobody but her seemed to want.

Pulling Judah's arm from his side, she bundled Jac into his embrace, making sure he had a firm grip before letting the little girl go. Refusing to look at him, Darby dropped a quick kiss on Jac's smooth forehead.

Darby smacked Jac's empty bottle into Judah's other hand and sent him a hard, tight smile. "My friend DJ says that having kids should be heavily regulated and subject to licensing. I've never agreed more with that statement than right now." She stared up into his beautiful face, confusion replacing anger. "I don't understand how someone so talented, who can put so much emotion into a building, can be so hard. And so cold."

Judah dipped his head so she could feel his breath on her ear, so she inhaled his unique scent of lemons and detergent and something earthy and sexy that made her want to bury her face in his neck and breathe him in. For a moment—a small infinitesimal moment—she imagined that she and Judah were a couple, that he was standing guard over his family, but the words that left his mouth shattered that image.

"This baby isn't mine."

Of course he'd say that.

"No, you just don't want her to be yours," Darby

muttered. "She should be good for about another half hour or so. After that, I hope she gives you hell. Bye now."

Judah's eyes hit hers and Darby felt their punch. All that gorgeous blue, that face and that body, wasted on a self-absorbed cretin.

Good luck, Jacquetta, you're going to need it, honey.

Three

Way to make friends and influence people. Judah watched the Duchess step toward the elevator, cursing when the doors closed on a froth of fabric. She was gone, and he should be glad.

Should being the operative word.

She'd just reamed him but instead of getting pissed he'd just been turned on... But, in his defense, she was smokin'.

She was also gone.

Judah shook his head. Well, that was that. Looking down at the little girl he held, he watched as her eyes fluttered closed and her mouth softened. She did look like him, Judah admitted. Then again, he and Jake both took after their dad and no one ever suspected that they were half siblings and not full blood brothers.

Judah thought he'd been the only casualty of Jake and Carla's illicit weekend spent together in his apartment but no, they always went a step further than necessary. Why light a Roman candle when you could detonate a bomb?

Judah felt the back of his throat burn. A year and a half had passed; how could the double betrayal still hurt so damn much? He ran his knuckle over Jac's flower-soft cheek. His pain, the fiery anger, he realized, wasn't only for him but also for Jacquetta. This little human, this doll-faced child, deserved better than two dysfunctional cretins as parents.

Judah used his free hand to pull his phone from the inside pocket of his jacket and scroll through his contact list. He hadn't dialed this number in so long, he hoped it was still operational.

The phone buzzed, beeped and started to ring.

Keep your cool, keep your cool...

"Judah, baby."

Her growly, sexy voice raised nothing more than red-hot anger. "What the hell, Carla? A baby? Are you insane?"

"I know it's a bit of a surprise, but I need you to take her for a while so I can finish this project."

"Let me think about that..." Judah replied, trying his utmost to keep his voice low. "No. A thousand times no! This isn't happening."

"It is." Carla's voice turned hard. "Either you or

your brother have to take her until I decide I want her back."

"Then call Jake, for God's sake! He's her father, not me! And don't you think one of you should've let me know I have a niece?"

"You made it very clear to both of us that you'd washed your hands of us."

"You talk as if I didn't find you naked in my bed, in a position I still can't get out of my head. Then you spilled the ugly details of our breakup to distract the press from finding out you were cheating on me with my much younger brother while I dealt with the mess Jake created."

Why had he even mentioned the past? Carla didn't care then, and she didn't care now.

"Call Rossi back or get Jake to come get his daughter," he said. "She. Is. Not. My. Problem."

"Do you think it would be wise of me to leave Jac with Jake? He's an addict with a felony record, thanks to you. He's not daddy material."

"Carla, you can't just dump a baby on me like she's a UPS parcel!" Okay, he'd borrowed that from the Duchess, but it applied. God, what had he seen in Carla? Oh, yeah, the sex had been phenomenal but like Turkish delight, she was best taken in small doses. "Come and get her, Carla."

"No," Carla replied. "I need some time. Just hear me out, please?"

He shouldn't, he really shouldn't, but his silence gave her room to speak.

"I have a new job, Bertolli is composing an opera and I am the lead character."

"Yeah, I heard. You are being cast against type."

"You are not the first to notice that. There have been a lot of insinuations already, about my past, you, my relationship with Bertolli."

"Which is?"

Carla didn't answer, which meant there was a very good chance she was sleeping with Bertolli. She was playing with fire. If word got out that she was sleeping with one of Italy's most conservative, outwardly faithful men, the country's favorite composer—a national treasure!—she would be labeled a sinful temptress and the press would eat her alive.

Judah walked to the end of the hallway and placed his hand on the floor-to-ceiling window. He looked down at the bustling streets of downtown Boston below, resting his forehead on the cool glass.

"There was a story recently, suggesting you are not her father. I cannot take the chance of the world finding out that Jake is Jacquetta's father and not you. It was enough of a scandal that I had a baby out of wedlock but if they find out about my liaison with Jake—"

"Affair."

"If they find out about Jake, that he is your brother and a heroin addict, that I had his baby not yours, the story will be on the front page of every tabloid from here to China. It will be a scandal and my con-

tract with the new production says I have to remain
scandal-free."

His heart bled. None of this had anything to do
with him. Jake and Carla had had sex in Judah's bed
and now they had to deal with the consequences of
their actions. He was in no way responsible for them
or the fruit of their loins.

Judah glanced down at the little girl and ignored
the tiny lump in his throat.

She could've been his...

No, he didn't want kids; he never had. He remembered having to change Jake's diapers, night after
night rocking him to sleep because their parents were
out on the town or simply out of town. For six years,
he'd been Jake's primary caregiver, the adult in the
house. He'd bought Jake clothes, made him meals,
packed his school lunches. As a twelve-year-old child
himself, Judah had stepped up to the plate and taken
on responsibility for another human being—because
his father and stepmother were useless—and Judah
had promised himself that he would never again put
himself in that position.

After a pregnancy scare in his early twenties, he'd
wanted a vasectomy, to take the issue off the table
permanently. But the doctor refused, telling Judah
he was too young, he might still change his mind.
Furious, Judah had vowed to find another doctor,
but then his career took off and he'd never found the
time to go back.

But he would. When he stopped being a monk,

he'd find another doctor. He was thirty-five, he hadn't changed his mind in ten years and he wouldn't be refused again. As a child, he'd raised his baby brother and he didn't want to raise another child.

A scholarship to college had been his exit out of that life and he still felt guilty for leaving six-year-old Jake behind. Despite Judah's attempts to keep tabs on his brother from afar, Jake was smoking weed by thirteen, fully addicted and boosting cars to feed his habit by sixteen. By eighteen, he was in juvie.

Never again would Judah put himself in the position of having to choose between his future and his obligations. So, no kids. And after a few relationships that went nowhere and Car Crash Carla, no commitment.

To anyone.

Ever.

Judah sucked in a calming breath. "I'm at the Sheraton, downtown Boston. Presidential suite. Get Rossi back here."

Carla pulled in a deep, ragged breath. "I tried to call him just before you called but his phone is off."

Judah gripped the bridge of his nose and cursed. "Make a plan, Carla."

Carla thought for a minute. "I'll call an agency, hire a nanny. They can send someone."

God, she was going to ask a stranger to pick up Jac? Now that was exactly the type of dick move his father and stepmother would've pulled. Judah felt the burn of intense anger. "No, Carla. You will come and get her. Yourself. Personally."

"I can't. It's just not possible." Carla spluttered her reply, making it sound like he'd asked her to become a nun.

"Jacquetta is your daughter, so you come and get her. It's not up for negotiation"

Carla finally ran out of expletives. "I'll come but I need some time."

"You've got a day. Be here in twenty-four hours or I'm going to be the one calling the tabloids, Carla."

"Judah, no! I am in Como, it will take more time than that."

"You should've thought about that when you played pass-the-parcel with your daughter," Judah said, not bothering to hide his annoyance. "Hurry up, Carla. The clock is ticking."

Judah disconnected the call and banged the face of his phone against his forehead. He released his own series of curses and looked down to see Jac sending him a wide-eyed look. "Your mom is something else, kid."

Jac blinked once, then again and then she smiled, revealing a gorgeous dimple and pink gums. Man, she was cute. And despite being passed from person to person, remarkably sanguine.

"So, I guess it's you and me for the next twenty-four hours."

Jac waved her pudgy arms in the air and kicked her legs.

"Glad you are on board with that program. It's been a while since I made bottles or changed diapers so if you can try not to be hungry or need a change in the next day or so, I'd be grateful."

Jac sent him what he was sure was a get-real look.

Judah walked her back to where the stroller stood, dropped her bag into the storage compartment and strapped her in. It had been years and years since he'd been in charge of anyone under two feet tall but he still instinctively knew what he was doing.

He could look after this child for a day. A day wasn't so long. Not when he compared it to looking after his brother day in and day out for six or so years.

This time around he was an adult and he had a voice. And he'd damn well use it.

After work the next afternoon, Darby sat down on the deep purple sofa in the showroom of Winston and Brogan and tucked a bright yellow cushion behind her back. While she loved color, and frequently approved of Jules's interior design choices, she simply did not like the industry's current obsession with eggplant. But Winston and Brogan were cutting-edge designers and they always reflected what was hot.

DJ squeezed Darby's shoulder before sitting down next to her, the diamond on the ring finger of her left hand so big Darby was sure she could see it from space. Jules's emerald was just as large, as valuable, as impressive. Darby's future brothers-in-law—one by law and both by love—were crazy about Jules and DJ respectively. Darby was happy they'd found their soul mates.

Hers was probably stuck up a tree or had been run over by an out-of-control bus. Or maybe there wasn't a man who would put up with a determined, driven, stubborn, type-A personality with fertility issues.

Jules placed a cup of tea on the white coffee table between them before taking the seat to DJ's left. DJ squeezed Darby's hand. "Sorry you didn't get the Grantham-Ford project, Darbs."

Darby forced a shrug. She hated to lose, even if it was to a Pritzker Prize winner. "It wasn't a surprise that Huntley got it. They'd be fools to pass up his design. It was magnificent."

So was Huntley, for a cold, hard jerk bucket.

Jules linked her hands around her knee. "And have they announced who will be his liaison between Huntley and Associates and the Grantham-Ford Foundation?"

Every architect in the city wanted a shot to work with Huntley, to be at his beck and call. Everybody but Darby. She'd seen the measure of the man last night and she was less than impressed.

"Don't care. It's an intern position and I'm not interested." She took the stack of paper DJ handed her and smiled. Financials. A discussion, then her dividend check. Yay.

DJ tapped the end of her pen against the stack of papers in her lap and cleared her throat. "Let's go through the financials first. Let's ignore page one and two and go straight to page three."

Darby flipped to the right page and saw the column detailing income and expenses. Compared to Jules's interior design income for the past six months, the architectural side of the business—Darby's side of the business—was trailing Jules's contribution by half. Up until this year, they'd been equal contributors, with DJ running the finances. It had been the perfect triangle, but now it looked like Darby's side was collapsing.

She took the check DJ handed her and looked at the total. Then she looked at DJ, wondering if she'd left off a zero.

"This is it?"

"Yes."

Well, hell.

DJ leaned forward, her eyes sober. "It wasn't a great quarter, it's tough out there. The interior design had a boost in income thanks to Noah employing Jules to do yacht interiors, and you had small jobs but nothing that brought in big money."

Darby stared at her check, her mind spinning. This check didn't come close to what she needed to pay for IVF. She'd have to put her buildings up for sale immediately, take what she could get for them. She might not even clear her costs, but it would free up the money. Any way she looked at it, she was moving backward, not forward. *Dammit.*

"There are other factors that contributed to a less than stellar year, Darby."

"Like?" Darby demanded.

"The rent on this building went up significantly—"

"We agreed we needed to be here, that this was the best place for us to be," Darby countered. "And that was only a ten percent increase." She skimmed the lines, looking for other anomalies. "The real reason we aren't growing is because I didn't bring in enough income."

The proof was there, in black and white. She hadn't been an equal contributor. She'd failed.

Darby didn't like to fail.

"I'll make it up to you. This next quarter, you'll see." She felt the need to apologize again. "I'm so sorry. You guys have worked so hard and I didn't pull my weight."

"Oh, for God's sake!" Jules muttered before sending her twin a hard look. "Can I hand you a hair shirt? Would that make you feel better?"

"But—"

"Who bankrolled this business, Darby?" Jules demanded, not giving Darby a chance to answer. "You did. You bought and fixed up that cottage and the profit you made paid our expenses for the first six months. Thanks to you, we didn't have to borrow money from Mom or Levi or a bank."

"The cost of renting the warehouse, the additional staff we've had to take on because we've expanded have all contributed to the drop in profits," DJ explained. "It's normal, Darby."

Darby looked at the profit-loss line and winced. "It's shocking."

DJ rolled her eyes. "You are such an overachiever, Darby. We can afford one less than stellar quarter. We still made a small profit."

But not enough, not nearly enough. From now on, Darby would be all over every project she could find. She'd work longer hours, take in as much work as she could. She had to make up the shortfall, and that meant doubling her income. She needed work, and lots of it.

"Oh, God, she's got that crazy look in her eye," Jules said. "You just flicked her competitive switch." She leaned forward, blue eyes pinning Darby to the seat. "We're in this together, Darby, so stop thinking this is your problem to solve. This is not a competition."

It was a refrain she'd heard all her life: you're too competitive, Darby. You can't treat anything as fun, Darby. You don't have to win at everything, Darby.

What no one understood was that being competitive was the way she was made. She couldn't remember a time when winning wasn't her goal.

One of her earliest memories was being on the playground, wanting to be the girl who could run the fastest, jump the longest, swing the highest. She excelled at all sports, was one of the most popular girls in school. She could remember dreading the results of tests, needing to achieve better grades than, well, everyone. Her report cards were all As and when she got her first C, in college, she'd been devastated.

Yes, she was competitive. Yes, she was driven. But, dammit, being both got results. She just had to refocus, redefine her goals. Do better, be better. Determination, her old friend, flowed through her, energizing her.

Darby Brynn Brogan had always produced the results and she would this time, too. Options, scenarios and plans buzzed through her brain.

DJ leaned her shoulder into Darby's. "Business is about troughs and highs, Darby, everything balances out in the end. I promise that Winston and Brogan is okay. The next cycle will be a lot better."

What if it wasn't? What if the economy worsened? She didn't deal in what-ifs, in maybes. She needed a plan to boost her side of the business. She needed work, a lucrative contract, and she knew one place where she could get one.

Judah Huntley had found his Boston-based architect. He just needed to be notified of the decision.

Four

After twenty-four hours of looking after Jac, Judah was hanging on to the end of his rope with his teeth. He was exhausted. He needed a shower and to sleep for a week.

Jac, he was certain, was as shattered as he was. She constantly needed to be reassured. She did this incredibly effectively, by crying incessantly. He'd changed her, fed her, held her, paced the room with her but the kid just cried.

And then she cried some more.

How had he done this as a child, a teenager? He must've had a guardian angel, some celestial being giving him guidance, because, God knew, the adults in the house hadn't been interested.

Judah pushed his hand into his hair and wondered,

again, where Carla was. He hadn't managed to reach her the past twelve hours. For the first ten of those hours, he hadn't been worried. She was in the air. But her flight landed two hours ago and she should have rocked up an hour ago. Judah tensed and re-minded himself that Carla had the attention span of a three-week-old puppy. She was easily distracted and being an hour late was nothing.

She could be stuck in a traffic jam or held up at customs. There were lots of reasonable explana-tions for her tardiness. She would get here eventu-ally. Late but begging him to forgive her, flashing that big smile and batting those enormous, expres-sive brown eyes.

He would forgive her anything if she would just take Jac and let him get some sleep.

Judah moved Jac up onto his shoulder, patted her little bottom and sighed when she let out another high-pitched wail. Why wasn't she asleep yet?

Hearing the buzz of the hotel room phone, Judah walked across the presidential suite and lunged for the phone before remembering he was holding a baby. Cursing, he tightened his hold on Jac, shook his head when her volume control went up and barked a greeting into the phone.

"Mr. Huntley you have a visitor—"

"Send her up," Judah muttered, banging the re-ceiver down. He rubbed Jac's back. "Your mommy is here, Jac. Think she can save us both?"

Jac's wail was his answer and he nodded. "I understand your worry. But if I know your mom, she will have brought a nanny with her and you'll be in safe hands."

Sleep was within his grasp. He looked across the room to the open door of the bedroom, sighing at the California king-size bed made up with fine Egyptian sheets and an expensive comforter. Ten minutes, maybe fifteen and he would be facedown in blessed quiet.

He liked quiet. He liked calm. Most of all, he liked sleep.

Judah went to stand by the front door. He would stay calm, he told himself. He would just hand Jac over, not engage with his volatile ex-lover—screaming and throwing stuff was Carla's favorite way to negotiate an argument—and then he'd lock the door behind him and strip off as he headed to his bedroom. He smelled like regurgitated milk since Jac had shown her disgust for the situation by vomiting all over his shirt. He should shower but he probably wouldn't; his need for sleep was too strong.

At thirty-five, he was too old to go for days without sleep. He was too old for drama, full stop.

Judah yanked open the door. All thoughts about keeping his cool disappeared. "I always thought you were unbelievably self-absorbed, but this behavior is beyond where I thought you would ever go. She's a little girl, Carla, not a doll— *Jesus*."

Judah blinked once, then again before lifting his free hand to rub his bleary eyes. But when he opened

his eyes again, the Duchess still stood in the doorway, her silver-gray eyes dominating her face.

Hoping against hope, Judah pulled her to the side
and stuck his head into the corridor. Nope, no feisty
Italian opera singer in sight. He looked down at his
watch. She was now an hour and a half late.

Judah was, not to put too fine a point on it, starting to worry. He needed to start making some calls.
Something about this entire situation felt wrong.

"This isn't a good time, Duchess."

The use of the nickname didn't impress her, but
Judah didn't care. He was too tired to deal with an
uptight blonde.

She stepped into the hallway, carefully shut the
door behind her and looked at the still-crying Jac.
"How long has she been upset?"

"Forever," Judah replied wearily. "I don't think
she's stopped crying."

"When did you last change her?" Darby demanded
in that crisp, no-nonsense, answer-me-dammit voice.
It turned him on. Why he had no idea. Maybe he
was nuts or maybe it was the fact that she was wearing tight black trousers that showed off her long,
lean body to perfection. The button-down shirt was
a shade of blue that reminded him of the sea around
Corfu and it nipped in at the waist, flashing a hint
of a bra the same color. He'd bet his fortune—a considerable amount—that her panties matched her bra.
The Duchess seemed the type.

Which reminded him, he couldn't keep calling her by that nickname. "Who are you?"

"Darby Brogan, architect. I'm a partner at Winston and Brogan," she replied. "Well, when?"

She was also waiting for a response and Judah used all his processing power to remember what she'd asked him. Right, changing a diaper. "A half hour ago."

Darby's perfectly arched eyebrows flew up toward her hairline. "Her last bottle?"

This was like the Spanish Inquisition. "Around the same time."

"Mmm."

What did that mean? Was that good or bad? Then he stopped caring because Darby, God bless her, reached for the baby. Relieved, Judah walked back into the living room, dropped his six-foot-three frame onto the closest sofa and stretched out.

Yeah, *this*. He fought to keep his eyes open. Rolling his head, he watched Darby take a small blanket from Jac's bag. He wasn't too tired to appreciate her long-legged and sexy-as-hell stride as she walked toward him. Using one hand, she spread the blanket on the chair and the little blood left in his brain ran south at the vision of that perfect ass bending over in front of him. He could easily imagine her naked, her blond hair touching the floor as she bent at the waist. High heels, a naughty smile—she was the girl in the posters he had on his bedroom wall as a teenager.

Okay, maybe he wasn't that tired.

Unaware that his mind was playing in the gutter, Darby placed Jac in the middle of the fabric square and quickly and efficiently bundled her up. Then she placed Jac against her chest and rhythmically patted the baby's back. Within twenty seconds, Jac's volume button was on low and then it was on mute.

Darby turned her back to him so he could see Jac's now peaceful face. "Is she asleep?"

She was, thank God. Thank Darby. "If I wasn't so damn grateful, I might be swearing at you right now. I've been trying to get her to go to sleep for, God, three hundred years."

"Babies are barometers, they need to know the adults in the room know what they are doing. You obviously don't." He was too tired to take any offense at her sarcasm. If only she knew…

Darby sat down on the chair, leaned back and eyed Judah. He felt like a bug under the microscope. Suddenly self-conscious, he wished he'd had the time to take a shower, to wash his face, to brush his hair. While Darby looked fresh and sexy and clean, dammit, he felt like he'd been dragged through a pigsty backward.

She didn't look impressed, and why should she? But why did he care whether he impressed her or not? And why was he so damn pleased to see her again?

Pushing aside his fall-at-her-feet gratitude for getting little Jac to stop crying, he admitted those silver-tinged thundercloud eyes enthralled him, and her take-control attitude made his mouth water. He was a driven guy, someone who instantly took control in tense situations and he generally didn't appreciate anyone muscling in on his turf. Yet Darby's take-charge attitude was not only refreshing, it was sexy as hell. She was the very last person he expected to knock at his door...

Which raised a point in his overtired brain. "Why are you here?"

Darby didn't waver, she didn't look away. "I want to work with you, for you."

Judah rubbed a hand over his face. "What the hell are you talking about?"

"You need a local architect to work with you on the Grantham-Ford project. I want to be that architect. Well?"

Huh. Darby was not only driven and direct, she was impatient, too. In between Jac's crying sessions, he'd lobbed a hundred and one things at his business manager, Jonathan, today. Jonno tossed as many back and the local liaison for Boston was way down their list of priorities. They'd get to it, they'd decided, in a day or two. But Darby had beaten them to it.

He couldn't employ her. He wanted her, naked and doing very unprofessional and non-architect-related things.

Man, what a mess. He didn't play where he worked. Ever.

Darby lifted her pretty nose. "I want the job."

He didn't like being bossed around, even if it was by a gorgeous blonde with the face of an angel. "In the past two days, I've had a maximum of four hours of sleep and I spent the whole of today and the best part of last night dealing with Jac. I'll tell you the same thing I told my business manager, I'll get to it when I get to it."

She looked both maternal and fierce, a perfect modern woman as she held a baby and kicked ass. "If you'd take the time to look at the designs I submitted, you will notice that my concept was more innovative than those of my competitors. I used modern building techniques, interesting materials, made it eco-friendly. I need—" Judah heard her voice hitch, heard the desperate note as she hesitated. "I deserve that job."

Interesting.

Something told him that Darby Brogan was here because she needed to be, not because she wanted to be. Oh, she probably thought he was a good architect, even a great one, but working with him, having his name on her résumé, wasn't why she was here… or it wasn't her primary reason for barging into his hotel room and throwing her demands at his head.

Somehow, she needed his help. Her desperation seemed more immediate than his name opening doors in a few months or years. Judah wondered if she needed the money the job commanded. Judah skimmed her outfit: designer pants, expensive top, stylish shoes. Discreet but tasteful jewelry. Darby didn't look like she needed cash.

"Don't bother interviewing the other competitors,

Judah, just hire me. I'll work harder for a lot longer, I'll give you my all."

The *all* he wanted from her involved her hair flowing down her back as he slid into her from behind, holding her breasts in his hands, his big body enveloping hers.

Judah ran a hand over his face and ordered his body to stand down. He was beyond tired; how could he possibly feel horny?

And his reaction to her was a very good reason *not* to hire her.

Darby shifted to the edge of the seat, her eyes never leaving his face. "I'm not married or involved so I'd be at your beck and call." *Oh, God, don't say that.* "I can give you references, show you other designs—"

A headache threatened to cleave his brain in two so Judah held up his hand and Darby, thank God, stopped talking. But five seconds later, she opened her mouth to talk again and he shook his head. He wasn't in a place to make any decisions about any projects or to think about hiring her. He was wickedly attracted to her and that fact complicated everything.

Before he made any decisions about bringing her into his life and company, he needed at least ten hours of sleep. He had to shut down this conversation before Darby hustled him into giving her a job.

Under normal circumstances *he* did the hustling, but nothing about the past thirty-six hours had been normal. Where the hell was Carla?

"I have a flash drive containing my portfolio—"

"Shut up, Darby."

Darby stopped talking and frowned.

Judah wanted to smile. He was pretty sure few people spoke to her in an obey-me-now tone of voice. Hell, he was impressed that she'd listened. But he absolutely knew she wouldn't remain silent for long.

Right, priority list: hand Jac over, make an appointment to meet with the very sexy—*stop thinking of her in those terms, Huntley!*—very smart and very determined Darby Brogan. And then sleep.

Picking up his phone, he dialed Carla's number. Instead of going straight to voice mail, her phone rang, and relief coursed through his body.

"Judah?"

He recognized that voice. Judah frowned, wondering why Carla's manager was answering her phone. "Luca? Why do you have Carla's phone? And where the hell is Carla, she should've been here already!"

Judah's voice rose, and he winced when he saw Darby's frantic gestures telling him to keep it down so he didn't wake Jac. Right, waking Jac would be a very bad thing.

"Are you telling me she's still in Italy?" Judah swore and gripped the back of his neck. "Okay, I will bring Jac to her."

"You can't, Judah. She can't care for Jac."

Of course, she couldn't, Carla had the mothering skills of a grasshopper. "She'll hire a nanny, do what she always does, pass her responsibilities on to someone else," Judah bitterly replied.

He shouldn't have trusted Carla, he should've just taken Jac back to Italy in the first place. The best predictor of future behavior? Past behavior.

"She's in the hospital, Judah. Her appendix burst and she collapsed."

What? No, she was about to storm through that door, and she'd throw a temper tantrum about how much he'd inconvenienced her. He stared at little Jac, frantically praying that he was mishearing Luca's words.

"She was rushed straight into surgery and she's now in ICU. We are waiting for her to come around."

"She's that ill?"

"No, it's just a precaution and also because ICU has better security than the general wards. She's expected to make a full recovery."

Judah felt adrenaline surge through his system. "I'll catch the next plane. Hell, I'll hire a private jet. We'll be there by morning." Judah scrambled to his feet and headed to the bedroom. He was about to pull open the door to the closet to start packing when Luca spoke again.

"Please don't, Judah."

Judah frowned, tightening his grip of the door to the closet. "And why not?"

"Judging by the press, you'd think she had a heart attack, not an appendectomy," Luca grumbled. "Do you think your entrance into the country, with the

baby, will go unnoticed? There is so much speculation, so much gossip... We don't need more." Luca's
sigh was deep and heavy.

Crap. Luca was right, the situation was volatile
enough without Judah's presence.

"I need you to keep Jacquetta for two weeks,
maybe three. Just until the press attention dies down.
Before Rossi left with her, we made Carla sign a
document stating that she was happy for you to have
temporary custody of Jacquetta." Luca's next words
were another shock. "And you need to keep your
brother away, as well!"

"I haven't spoken to Jake for eighteen months,
Luca, you know that. I don't know where he is,"
Judah retorted.

"The press is reporting that he is in the area and
that he's been in contact with Carla, but that could
just be rumormongering. The last person I need here
is her drug-addicted ex-lover."

Definitely rumormongering. "Don't you think
you are overreacting? They spent *one* weekend together, Luca."

"Judah, it wasn't one weekend. Carla was doing
an eight-week stint at the Met and you said she could
stay at your place while she was in New York. Your
brother moved in three days after she did, the week
after you left for Sydney. They lived together for
three months."

It was a blow, but just a sideswipe, not a full-on
punch. Did the duration of their affair matter? One

weekend? Three months? Judah didn't think so. Betrayal was betrayal.

When Judah didn't speak, Luca spoke again. "I'm asking you to keep Jacquetta, Judah. Please?"

"Why should I, Luca? Why should I flip my world upside down for her?" Judah demanded.

"Because you loved Carla once? Because Jac has nowhere else to go for the next two weeks? Because I need to keep that baby out of the limelight and I need you, as her uncle, to help me do that."

Crap. "Dammit, Luca. I thought I was done with the drama."

Luca managed a small snort. "As long as Carla is in your life, you never will be, my friend."

And wasn't that a solid-gold truth.

Mason, tallying receipts in his head because that was more fun than using a calculator, looked up as the door chime jangled.

It was four o'clock on a snowy winter's afternoon and he hadn't had a customer in over two hours. He'd let his staff go home an hour ago and Mason considered telling the bundle consisting of a heavy coat and a thousand scarves that he was closing but figured he could give out a cup of coffee before he sent the person back into the snow.

Mason watched as the cap came off first, revealing bright blond hair—hair he'd buried his face in. Blue eyes, pink cheeks, that luscious mouth he'd been—was still—addicted to.

Callie.

Mason gripped the edge of the counter, fighting the twin waves of fury and desire. He hadn't seen or heard from her since New Year's Eve, nine weeks and two days ago. She hadn't stepped into his coffee shop. He hadn't seen her car driving around. He'd noticed that her house was shut up tight.

He'd been annoyed that evening—competing with a ghost wasn't any fun—and he'd expected her to run over to his house and apologize. She'd run but in a direction he never expected.

"Had fun wherever the hell you went?"

Callie kept her coat on as she walked over to the register, her eyes locked on his. "I did, actually. I went to Thailand, then Bali."

"Good for you." Mason pushed the words out between gritted teeth. "A postcard would've been nice. Or, you know, an explanation."

"You left that party without a word, you didn't call. When you didn't bother to connect with me, I assumed we were done."

He'd been angry and annoyed and jealous, but done?

Oh, hell, no.

When he heard that she'd left for Southeast Asia, he'd been on the point of caving, going after her. Furious with her, and himself, he'd gone on one or two dates but, because he was an idiot for this woman in front of him, he couldn't take up even one of the many offers of sex that he'd received.

He'd been celibate but… He took a closer look at Callie's eyes and knew something had changed within her. She looked relaxed, confident, assured…

And Mason somehow knew she'd crossed off another item on her bucket list: sex in the sun. Mason ground his teeth together. He wasn't going to ask.

He was not going to ask…

"Who was he?" he asked.

"Who was who?"

He wanted to know what happened in Southeast Asia. Because, God, any fool could see that something had.

Mason opened his mouth, then shut it. He had no claims on her, had no right to be jealous. There was nothing more between them than hot sex, a raging attraction. He had no hold on Callie. They didn't owe each other exclusivity. Neither of them wanted commitment.

They'd made the rules and now he had to play by them.

Callie placed her hands over his fingers, which were flat on the counter, and Mason felt like she'd plugged him into a power source. God, he'd missed her.

Callie peered past his shoulder, trying to look into the tiny kitchen behind him. "Who else is here, Mace?" she asked.

He looked over his shoulder, not quite understanding the question. "Uh…no one?" Why was she asking? What did that have to do with anything?

"Good." Callie smiled, lifted her hands to her coat and started to undo the buttons. "So, want to pick up where we left off?"

Mason barely heard her words because, instead of a sweater and jeans, Callie's slow striptease revealed a black lacy bra and an equally lacy triangle at the juncture of her thighs. Surely, this could not be happening.

Mason ground his teeth together again and watched as Callie's designer coat fell to the floor.

Black lace lingerie and thigh-high boots.

Holy, holy crap.

Mason knew his eyes were bugging out. He could not believe that straitlaced, slightly prudish Callie Brogan was nearly naked in his coffee shop while the snow pelted down outside. Somebody could arrive, somebody might drive past...

He really didn't care.

Mason boosted himself up and over the counter, grabbing Callie's hand and marching her to the door. He flipped the lock, gave the deserted landscape a quick once-over. The chance of discovery, thanks to the snow, was minimal.

He wouldn't make love to her out here but if someone drove past and saw a nearly naked Callie Brogan, in black lace and boots, being kissed within an inch of her life, then it was her own damn fault.

She should never have left him; she should've come back sooner. He wanted to yell at her, kiss her, take her up against the door...

He never wanted to miss her as much as he had missed her ever again. A life without Callie Brogan in it was a colorless place...

Callie wound her arms around his neck and brushed her mouth against his. "Kiss me, Mace. I've missed you."

Five

Darby placed Jac in her stroller before walking across the penthouse suite to the open door of Judah's bedroom. Judah stood by the closet, his shoulder pressed into the door, looking utterly played out. Yes, she wanted the job as his local architect and she'd had no intention of leaving until she had his assurance that the job was hers, but right now, he looked shattered.

Her heart swelled with sympathy. Judah, she suspected, didn't like surprises and he liked to steer his own ship. Discovering that he had a child he hadn't known about was a complication that would be totally out of his comfort zone.

Despite the discussion held in rapid Italian, Darby sensed Jac was staying with him. He was either feeling utterly out of his depth or frustrated beyond belief. Possibly both. With no warning and little thought, Judah's ex had backed him into a corner. A guy like Judah—strong, alpha, confident—didn't do corners.

"Hey."

Judah's head shot up and she saw emotion dancing through his eyes. Fear, sadness, worry. Yep, that conversation had rocked his world. Those eyes, all that ink blue, held confusion and anger and, though he would never admit it, pain.

His body was drool worthy, and she was in awe of his talent. But her attraction to his mind was what made her earth tilt. This visceral, intense, knee-shaking need to know what drove him, what scared him, what motivated him—it terrified her and made her take a few mental steps back.

She had a business to bolster, money to earn, a baby to breed. She couldn't afford to be distracted by a tired hot luscious man whose depths ran deeper than the Mariana Trench.

"I was expecting Carla to collect Jac but she's in the hospital," Judah explained, sounding tired beyond belief. "I've got to look after her, take care of her for two weeks."

Well, he was Jac's father. That was what dads did.

A part of Darby, a big part, hoped that when Judah got over his shock at having a daughter he'd fight to be part of Jac's life on an ongoing basis, that the little girl would have at least one parent who cared about her. But Judah was a man always on the go, his work had him living from city to city, job to job. She doubted Jac would find any stability with him.

Darby shook her head, confused. Here she was, someone who would be a good mom and unable to have kids. Yet Carla and Judah didn't want the beautiful baby they had.

It was so unfair...

Familiar with this negative thought process, Darby knew she needed to leave, to find some distance and perspective. Being around Jac made her sad about what she couldn't have. It didn't help that she wanted Jac's dad, too.

"Okay, well, if you can let me know a suitable time for me to be interviewed..."

Judah straightened and walked over to her. Darby couldn't yank her eyes from his. He stopped in front of her, so close she could feel his heat, smell his deodorant, see that he had a tiny scar on the corner of his left eye and another on his chin. His fingers gripped her hips and a tremor skittered through her. If she lifted herself onto her toes, just a little, her mouth would be aligned with his, she would know his taste.

Don't do it, Darby. Bad, bad, dreadful *idea.*

Judah's other hand snaked around her back, splaying across the top of her butt as he gently pulled her toward him. Her breasts scraped his chest, her nipples puckering against the lace of her bra. She wanted his mouth there, she realized, shocked. She wanted him tugging on her, trailing his lips across her naval and down to where she was wet and throbbing.

Potential boss alert! Unprofessional! Ding! Ding! Ding!

Darby ignored her brain's loud screech and kept her eyes locked on his, seeing images of what could be in his eyes.

While he would never force her to do anything she was uncomfortable with, he wouldn't be a gentle lover. He'd demand everything from her, make her experience every last drop of pleasure. She wanted that, wanted to be intensely, absolutely in the moment with him, experiencing the mind-stealing, heart-shattering bliss she suspected he could give her.

Judah covered her mouth with his, and as she expected, colorful fireworks exploded behind her eyes.

For the first time ever she felt, God help her, like she'd stepped into an alternate reality where nothing could touch her, where this man and his mouth and his broad hands moving over her body, felt good and…right.

Under her hands, his pecs were hard and his stomach flat, the ridges suggesting an impressive six pack. His hips were narrow but his erection, pushing into her stomach, was hard and long and thick. His mouth never lefts hers, that tongue doing wicked things to her. He fed her kisses in a way that each stroke, each slide left her hungry for more.

Their behavior was so far beyond unprofessional it wasn't even funny…

Darby pulled back, pulled her bottom lip between her teeth and dragged her reluctant hands off his body. "That was, uh… Dammit."

Judah lifted a strand of her hair that was stuck to the corner of her mouth. Instead of pushing it behind her ear, he wrapped the strand around his index finger.

Leave, Brogan.

But Darby stayed where she was, an inch from him, fighting the urge to go in for more, knowing that it would be deeper, harder, more intense. She also knew that if she did, the chances of them making use of that very big and comfortable-looking bed were sky-high.

Avoid the bed, Brogan.

"I really should go," Darby said. This time her feet cooperated, and she managed to put a good half foot between them and her hair slipped from his finger.

Judah didn't say anything, he just stood there and looked at her, his eyes conveying exactly where she should go and what she should do when she got there. His bed and naked.

His message wasn't that difficult to decipher.

Ignore it, ignore him. Be an adult, Darby.

Sex was easy but the chance of working with a world-famous architect who paid higher than normal rates didn't come along daily. Or even every year.

Darby walked back into the sitting room, feeling Judah's eyes on her back. In the hallway, she picked up her bag, pulled it over her shoulder, and lifted her hair up and off her neck, allowing it to fall down her back. Taking a deep breath, she turned to face him, hoping her smile was polite rather than please-take-me-now.

Judah's expression remained inscrutable and she wished she had a small idea of what he was thinking. "So, I really hope to hear from you soon. I'd just like to reassure you that you'd never regret giving me the job."

"I know I won't."

Darby blinked, frowned and tipped her head to the side. "Sorry... What?"

"You've got the job."

Before her brain could assimilate that thought, Judah spoke again. "And just so we are clear about what just happened, I kissed you before I made the offer. I don't mess with my colleagues or employees." Judah's voice was all controlled determination.

"I see," Darby replied. It was all she could say since she was still fighting the urge to slap her mouth against his and take up where they left off.

She knew they couldn't sleep together or have any sort of affair. There were too many risks—how would she know if he was impressed with her work or her rusty mattress skills? It was always awkward when it ended and ending it with her *boss* would be even more so.

So why did she still feel like a hot, fast orgasm or two would be worth the fallout? That mouth. That strong tanned neck. Those very broad muscled shoulders...

Focus, Brogan.

"Thank you," Darby said when her overstimulated brain finally kicked into gear.

She had the job, but she still craved the man.

"There is one proviso," Judah muttered, rubbing the black stubble on his jaw.

Oh, God, what now?

"I want help with the baby. Due to the press interest around Carla and by association Jac, I need to lie low, keep out of the limelight. I'll give you the job if you help me out with the kid. I'll stay here, in Boston, for the next two weeks. You can work with me on the new art museum and together we look after Jac. And if you agree to do that, I'll give you another five percent."

Darby made a swift calculation in her head. If he did that, she'd boost Winston and Brogan's bottom line. She would be working with someone she respected as well as looking after a baby, two of her favorite things. How could she refuse?

Except her competitive nature never would allow her to accept without pushing the envelope a little further.

"Okay," Darby said, keeping her tone cool. "And to compensate for the extra hours, I want a flat daily fee for looking after Jac." She named a figure, saw Judah's eyes widen and expected him to bargain her down to half that amount. Even at the bargain price, she'd be adding a significant amount to her IVF fund.

To her astonishment, and delight, Judah nodded and waved his hand. "Fine."

He whirled around, stomped back into the living room and Darby followed him. At the door to his bedroom, he turned. "But that means you start now, you're on kid duty tonight. Do not wake me unless Jac has arterial bleeding and is about to spontaneously combust from a high temperature. 'Night."

Darby watched, openmouthed, as he slipped inside his bedroom. The door slammed in her face.

Well, okay then. At what he was paying her, she couldn't refuse. Besides, she could deal with Jac, she'd had tons of experience with babies.

Three hours later, when Jac was still crying, Darby wasn't so sure.

The next morning, in the coffee shop attached to the hotel, Darby took her first sip of her third cup of coffee and glanced at Jac, who was finally sound asleep in her stroller.

It had been a hell of a night.

The door to the shop opened and Darby looked up to see Jules and DJ walking into the too-early-to-be-busy shop. They stopped at the counter and ordered their beverages before sauntering her way. Darby was relieved to see her large leather tote bag over Jules's shoulder. Darby was still in yesterday's clothes and desperately needed a shower and a change.

The unwelcome image of Judah sharing her shower,

his big body slick with soapsuds, flashed behind her eyes and she frowned.

Damn him for kissing her last night. Now that she knew how his lips felt on hers, how talented that mouth was, how his big hands felt skating over her hips, down her spine, she'd been bombarded with X-rated images all night. It was like she'd fallen into an erotic novel.

It had been a night short on sleep and long on frustration.

"I need sex," Darby muttered, blushing when she realized that she had not only said the words out loud, but DJ and Jules had also heard her.

Jules grinned. "We can highly recommend sex."

"Shaddup." Darby yawned, covering her mouth with her hand. "I got the job as Huntley's local liaison."

DJ pointed at beautiful Jac. "It looks like you got more than that." DJ shook her head. "I should be shocked that you went to snag a job but ended up with a baby, but I'm not."

"How on earth did you end up looking after a baby, Darby?" Jules asked.

Darby couldn't resist running her hand over Jac's sweet soft curls. "Judah and I struck a deal. I get the job, as long as I help him with little Jac here."

She could see the concern in their eyes, but it was DJ who lobbied the first question. "He doesn't have enough money to hire a nanny?"

Darby leaned forward and told them, quietly and

quickly, what she could about Jac's arrival in Judah's life.

"I went online last night. Carla is stable, but the press is looking for any angle. They're already reporting on Judah being here in Boston. Judah wants to keep Jac out of the public eye. He's paying me extra, both as his architect and as his nanny, to help him out with her. It's a good deal."

Jules narrowed her eyes. "It's an *unusual* deal."

Darby felt a wave of exhaustion sweep over her. "It's just business, Jules."

Well, apart from that kiss last night.

That was far and away the best kiss she'd ever had, both sweet and sexy, hot enough to blister but tender enough to soothe. If he was that good a kisser, he'd be a dynamite lover.

DJ snapped her fingers in front of Darby's nose. "Hey, you! Where did you go?"

Oh, don't mind me, I was just sliding all over a big and bold Judah, exploring that fantastic body with my teeth and tongue.

Yeah, if she said that out loud they'd have a field day.

DJ released a half snort, half laugh. "Oh, God, though it's been years, I recognize that foggy look in your eyes."

Darby fussed with Jac's blanket so she didn't have to meet DJ's eyes. "I have no idea what you are talking about."

"Like hell you don't. You've had a crush on him for months."

Darby felt like the roots of her hair were on fire. "I have not," she spluttered, glaring at her best friend. "There's a distinct difference between admiring his work and crushing on him." She'd been crushing on his buildings for years; her attraction to the man was a recent development. Again, not something they needed to know. "Why are we using that word? How old are we, thirteen?"

DJ's smile turned wicked. "Then would you care to explain why you showed me a photo of him running shirtless on some beach?"

Trust DJ to remember that. Darby scowled. "You are so annoying."

DJ laughed. "I try." She picked up Darby's phone and swiped her thumb across the screen. "Jules, let me see if I can find the picture she showed me."

Dammit, why had she never put a code on her phone? Darby snatched her phone back and tossed it into her tote bag. She glanced at her watch, saw it was later than she thought. Although she'd left a note for Judah telling him where she was, along with her phone number, she thought it was time she returned to his hotel suite. They had much to discuss and she really wanted that shower.

"Thanks for bringing me my stuff," Darby said, standing up. She dropped a kiss on Jules's cheek and was about to do the same to DJ when she saw Judah step into the coffee shop.

All the moisture in her mouth dried up as his eyes slammed into hers. Darby immediately forgot about Jules and DJ, even little Jac, as she fell into that vat of dark blue. In his eyes, she saw everything she wanted him to do to her...

From a place far away, she heard DJ mention something about the air fizzing with electricity and that she needed a fan.

Darby gave herself a mental slap and dropped back into her seat, keeping her eyes on Judah as he flashed a smile at the barista behind the counter. She'd expected a bleary-eyed, rough-looking, moody architect. But the man paying for his coffee was bright eyed, clean shaven and impeccably dressed. He'd tucked a white shirt into a pair of caramel-colored chinos, topped the shirt with a sage-colored cashmere sweater, sleeves pushed back to reveal a very expensive watch and muscled forearms.

Judah walked over to where they were sitting, stopped next to the stroller and looked down. The tip of his finger glided across Jac's downy head. For a guy who didn't want kids, he was very comfortable with the baby.

"Morning. How was your night?" Judah asked her, placing his hand on the back of the empty chair next to hers.

Because she couldn't kiss him or feel that small smile against her lips, she glared at him. "Sleepless."

"You have to suffer to earn the ridiculous fees you charge," Judah murmured, taking the seat next to hers. Not waiting to be introduced, he held out his hand to Jules and then to DJ.

They had their men and were both stupidly in love, so it was very annoying to watch her smart, confident, kick-ass partners melt at his feet. He wasn't that good-looking.

Okay, he was, but really? She expected better from them.

Darby bent down and pulled her laptop from the storage area under the stroller and placed it on the table in front of her. She lifted the lid and sent Jules and DJ a pointed look. "I'm sure you want to get to the shop."

DJ shook her head. "Actually, we don't. Since we hired Maribeth as office manager, we are a lot more flexible. We can sit here for a bit."

Darby glared at her friend, who just smiled back. Oh, yeah, they'd have words later. Ignoring her, Darby turned her attention back to Judah. "We should go back upstairs. We have a lot to discuss."

"Not before I finish my coffee," Judah replied.

Why was no one listening to her? Irritated, Darby pulled up a document on her computer and angled the laptop so Judah could see the screen.

He squinted at her, shook his head, still damp from the shower, and gestured to the colorful screen. "What the hell is that?"

"A plan of action," Darby replied, ignoring the groans coming Jules and DJ.

Jules leaned forward, looked at the screen and

sent Judah a commiserating look. "That's a hell of a list. Sympathies."

Really, whose side was Jules on? Not Darby's, obviously.

Before Darby could utter a scathing retort, DJ changed the subject. "Judah, I understand that you know my fiancé? Matt Edwards?"

Judah smiled, and Darby's internal organs started to fizz. Man, he was seriously delicious. His smile should be registered as a weapon. Unfortunately, or maybe fortunately, it wasn't directed at her.

"Human rights lawyer? I met him in Amsterdam. How is he?"

"Good." Excitement crossed DJ's face. "I'll be staying with him in The Hague. He can't get away right now so I'm going there."

"Send him my regards."

Mischief danced in DJ's eyes. "If you are planning on staying in Boston for a while and you want a more private place to stay, you're welcome to use my apartment."

What? No! Darby widened her eyes at DJ, silently begging her to rescind her offer.

"DJ has the apartment over the garage at our childhood home, the house Darby still shares with our older brother, Levi," Jules explained to Judah. "We all live in the Lockwood Country Club gated community. I'm surprised Darby hasn't mentioned it to you since you are trying to keep a low profile."

I didn't mention it because I need distance from

the sexy architect, my new boss. I don't *need to live within shouting distance of him.*

"I don't think that would work for Judah," Darby protested. Of course, it would but it sure as hell wouldn't work for her!

"It makes sense, Darby. You can use the study in the house as your office base and nobody will mind if you bring that gorgeous creature—" DJ nodded to Jac, still asleep in her stroller "—to work."

Was DJ matchmaking? If so, Darby was going to kill her, best friend or not. The attraction between her and Judah was crazy enough without forcing them to be in super close proximity.

"Through my fiancé, Noah Lockwood, I'll arrange for you to become a temporary member of the Lockwood Country Club, Judah. There's golf, obviously, but also a state-of-the-art gym, an Olympic-size swimming pool, and if you get swamped and need help with Jac, there are experienced nannies on call that you can hire by the hour, or day," Jules offered.

Oh, God, two against one.

Before Darby could think of another reason why Judah shouldn't move next door to her—why wasn't her brain working?—Judah spoke. "That's a very kind offer, which I'll gratefully accept."

Oh, damn. Oh, hell.

Darby closed her eyes and shook her head. She knew Judah was intelligent, but this wasn't a smart plan. Levi rarely spent any time at home. She and

Judah would mostly have the big house to themselves. Because it was inside a sprawling neighborhood, with acres of greenery between the houses, they could go for days, weeks, without anyone seeing them.

They could have a roaring red-hot affair and nobody would know about it.

As one, DJ and Jules stood up. Darby glared at them. *Yeah, mess with my life and plans and then go. Nice.*

Jules just grinned at her, but DJ walked around the table and bent down to give Darby a hug. "I'll see you in a few months. Love you."

Darby hugged her friend back. Turning her mouth, she whispered in DJ's ear, "You are so dead."

Darby felt DJ's smile. Her whisper brushed her ear. "You are so going to get laid. Let me know what you decide about the IVF. In the meantime, have some fun with Mr. Sexy. After all, it might be the last sex you get before becoming a single mom."

Callie sat in the corner of her big sofa, her legs tucked up under her, and wondered when the nor'easter would wind down.

She'd been back in the States for forty-eight hours yet she was already tired of the cold heavy damp snow. It was a minor miracle that she hadn't frozen to death as she'd run from her car to Mason's coffee shop yesterday. And thank the Lord she hadn't crashed her car or spun out; she would be the talk of Boston if the emergency services team found her dressed in just a coat and sexy underwear.

It had been a stupid thing to do, and she'd kill her daughters if she found out they'd braved an ice storm to seduce a man, but Callie had been unable to wait. She'd needed to know whether Mason still wanted her, whether her time away had killed his desire for her.

Judging by his passionate response, not even a little bit.

For her part, from the moment she'd touched down in the States, she'd been unable to think of much else except seeing Mason, touching him, re-exploring that powerful body, inhaling his scent, having his words and voice and hands and mouth touching her skin.

Callie couldn't even blame her impatience on sexual frustration since she'd seen a little action while she was away. She smiled. Callie Brogan, society doyenne, Ray Brogan's wealthy, once-proper widow using *seeing* and *action* in the same sentence.

Callie picked up her phone and scrolled through her pictures of Thailand, stopping on the photo of a blond man holding a beer in his big hand. That hand had cradled her face, caressed her body and, for one night, she'd enjoyed his touch. She'd met him on the beach in Ko Tao and had slept with him two nights later.

It had been nice sex, fun sex…

Callie scrolled on and stopped at the image of a black-haired man, younger than her but not by much.

She'd been in Candidasa and she and Greg had spent the week together before she'd allowed him to kiss her, to indulge in some heavy petting under a full moon.

She was fifty-five years old and she'd now slept with three and a half men. Two and half in the last two months. Callie was both proud and flabbergasted but not ashamed.

Maybe she should be, but she sure as hell wasn't.

Her heart had been in hibernation for so long, her libido for even longer, and Mason had yanked her out of her cave. She hadn't realized it when she impulsively booked a flight to Southeast Asia but she needed to go away to meet herself, to find out who she was and what she wanted.

She missed her husband, she probably always would, but in Thailand, she'd finally accepted that Ray was gone, that her actions didn't—couldn't—affect him. Her life was her own.

As was her body. She could sleep with whomever she pleased.

It took a little time, a lot of honesty and facing the best and worst of herself before she came to the profound acceptance of the fact that she was allowed to question her life and her beliefs. That she could not only explore herself, her sexuality and her future but she *owed* it to herself to do exactly that. She was the only one she had to consult, the only person to please.

She also owed it to herself to find out who she was and what she wanted.

She had money, lots of it, and she wanted to use her wealth in ways that mattered, ways that would honor Ray and the businessman he'd been. She had thoughts about providing seed money to fund micro-businesses in developing countries; her business degree and being Ray's right-hand person reassured her that she could spot a good idea when she saw one. There were lots of options, many places and people who needed her help. She'd never be bored again.

But how did she really feel about that big demanding rebellious tattooed math geek who—what was the expression Darby used?—set Callie's panties on fire?

Was Mason just a fling, a bridge from her old life to her new one, or was he simply someone or something different? Was he her rebellion? Was he just good sex? Or maybe just a total contrast to Ray, who'd been so safe, so stable?

Yesterday had been anything but safe and stable; her actions had been outright madness. Okay, the coat and the sexy lingerie hadn't been necessary, or even clever, in a snowstorm, but seeing the shock on Mason's face had been worth the risk of hypothermia.

After slapping her bare butt against the glass door of his coffee shop and kissing her brainless, he'd hoisted her over his shoulder and jogged back to his cramped office, where he'd taken her on top of his keyboard, papers, pens and receipts.

It had been wild and sexy and the very opposite of nice.

After her two Thailand encounters, she now suspected Mason was the only man who could turn her core molten, who could whip her up to a point where she begged, who could turn her into a wild, crazy, on-fire-for-him woman.

Callie sighed. She no longer wanted the sex she'd had in Thailand: gentle, considerate…nice sex. She wanted the heart-pumping, soul-destroying, clothes-tearing sex she'd had with Mason yesterday.

She'd always love Ray, would always hold on to the memories of him, but now the only person she could imagine in her bed, in her life, was that surly annoying man down the road.

But how could she have Mason and the new life she needed? She wanted her freedom, but dammit, she wanted Mason, too.

Something was going to have to give. She'd have to compromise. But what would she have to lose?

Her freedom and her future or Mason?

Six

"Interesting friends."

Darby turned back to Judah and nodded. They *were* interesting—and very damn annoying. "Don't feel obligated to take DJ up on her offer of the apartment."

Judah leaned back and laced his fingers over his hard belly. "I never feel obligated to do anything. But I think it's a practical solution to my tabloid press problem." He tipped his head to the side. "But you don't think so and I'm curious as to why not."

He hadn't asked a question, so Darby didn't respond, choosing to look at her laptop screen instead.

"Could it be because you are worried you won't be able to keep your hands off me?"

Heat rocketed into Darby's cheeks, across her

forehead, down her neck. But embarrassment—and him putting his finger on that solid-gold truth—wasn't a good enough reason to let his statement remain unchallenged. "I could kill myself jumping off your ego."

Darby liked the way his face remained inscrutable while laughter sparked in those ink-blue eyes. Her eyes dropped to his lips and she remembered the taste of him, his assured way of holding her, his confidence in what he was doing and how to do it. He would take control in bed and the thought excited her. A lot.

Of course, she was worried about being able to keep her hands off him. He was spectacular.

She was not going to get hot and bothered. *Not, not, not.* She could not afford to bring that much drama into her life.

Jac snuffled and Darby sent her a fond, if exasperated, look. The baby had kept Darby awake for most of the night and now, when it was time to wake up, she was dead to the world.

Judah, in contrast, looked refreshed, smelled like an orchard of something citrusy and was firing on all cylinders. She was…

Not.

Darby pushed her shoulders back and straightened her spine. There was nothing she could do about her appearance right now. It was more important to get her life—their lives—on track. Throughout the night, whenever Jac settled down enough to allow

Darby a couple of minutes to work, she started list-
ing the steps they'd need to take to make the next
couple of weeks a success.

Or at the very least, avoid neglecting Jac, failing
the art museum project or killing each other.

Darby turned her attention back to her laptop
screen and the spreadsheet she'd compiled during
the night. She immediately felt calmer. With her lists,
she could achieve world domination if she wanted.

Right now, her main aim was to bring a certain
famous architect over to her way of thinking.

Darby turned the laptop and moved her chair so
they both had a good view of the screen. His wonderful scent and the warmth from his body flipped
her switch. Shaking her head, she forced herself to
ignore the lust river coursing through her body. This
was about work, not play.

Judah gestured to her monitor with his coffee cup.
"What's this?"

"A plan of action."

Judah leaned forward, frowning. "It's all color
coded."

"It's pretty but functional. Pink is Jac related,
green is the color I allocated to the art museum
project, aqua is your personal business, purple is
mine—"

Judah looked at the screen again. "Why have you
booked a day off next week?"

Darby flushed, heat coursing through her. Whether
she decided to try IVF now or later, she'd need eggs,

and thinking that her dividend check would be bigger, she'd made an appointment and paid the deposit to have her eggs harvested.

The urge to tell Judah that she was infertile, that there was a strong possibility she'd never be able to hold her own child, was both strong and strange. She rarely shared her gynecological history with anyone. It wasn't anyone's business but her own.

Darby looked at his profile and for the first time in a long time—years and years and years—she wanted to tell someone—*him*—that she felt inadequate. Crazy. Why him and why now? All she knew about Judah Huntley was that he was a supremely talented architect, that he wasn't a pushover and that he kissed like a dream.

She was simply tired and not thinking straight. Once she got a few hours' sleep, she would feel normal again.

She hoped.

"You didn't answer my question."

And she had no intention of doing so. Darby tapped the touch screen and another list came up. "This is everything I could think of that needs to be accomplished. If you think of anything, you can add it here. I've set up an account so we can share these and I've emailed you the authorization codes."

Judah looked from the screen to her and back to the screen. "When did you do this?" he demanded.

"Last night. In between Jac's bouts of misery."

Darby saw his puzzled look and lifted her hands. "What?"

"You are a spreadsheet freak. I have never seen anything like it in my life."

Darby wasn't sure if his statement was a mockery or a compliment. "I like lists. They keep me organized."

Judah leaned back in his chair and cocked his head. "Oh, I think you like them because they make you feel like you are in control."

She *was* in control. There was no "feeling" involved. Darby dismissed his observation with a wave of her hand. She'd always known what she wanted and how to get it. One just needed to be prepared and to persevere. Most situations could be solved by making lists and breaking a big project down into manageable tasks.

Unfortunately, no matter how many lists she made, she couldn't get her body to cooperate with creating a child. And it was just as impossible to convince potential life partners to stick around after explaining that effort and money would be needed for her to start a family and that failure was a very real possibility.

Enough now, Darby. You're on a solo journey. Get used to it.

Darby forced her attention back to her list. "We need to make a couple of decisions about Jac. The first is that I would like to get her checked out by a doctor. I think she might have an ear infection and that's why she's not sleeping."

"She could also be feeling unsettled because she's in a strange place with strange people and she has no clue what's going on," Judah suggested, and Darby heard the annoyance in his voice.

"Sure, that's a possibility, but she also thumped her fist against her ear and I remember one of the babies I looked after doing that and it turned out she had an ear infection." Darby, unable to sit this close to him and not touch him, shifted to put some distance between them.

"You looked after babies when you were a kid?"

Darby nodded. After she'd been given the news that she might never have her own children, she'd sought out babies, needing to be around what she thought she couldn't have. Being told no, that she couldn't do something, was like waving a red rag at a bull. Her stubborn, determined nature immediately kicked into higher gear.

Thank God she hadn't had a boyfriend in her teens; she might have had unprotected sex with him just to prove to herself that she could get pregnant.

Was that why she was strongly considering IVF? Because someone had told her no?

Uncomfortable with the direction of her thoughts, she moved back to the list. "I've made an appointment for ten thirty with a pediatrician working out of the same practice as my doctor and I gave him your billing information," Darby told him. "I'd like to go home first to shower and change. While I'm doing that, you can look over DJ's apartment and see if it will suit you."

Judah placed his coffee cup on the table in front of him and scanned her list again. "Are you always this obsessively detailed?"

She wanted to lie, to play it down, but he'd find out the truth sooner rather than later. "Yes."

Judah grinned. "God help me." Turning to face her, he lifted his hand to brush her hair back from her forehead. His eyes slammed into hers and Darby saw amusement mixed with concern in all that blue. "Take a breath, Brogan, don't worry so much."

She wasn't worried, she was organized. Being organized stopped her from being worried. It kept her on track to reach her goals, made sure she achieved what she set out to do. Why couldn't people understand that?

"I'm not worried. I just want to do my job." Darby's body stiffened with tension.

The corners of Judah's mouth lifted. "And that job would be world domination?"

Oh, now he was just mocking her.

Darby felt her spine snap straight and she cursed the blush she could feel in her cheeks. "Are you prepared to consider what I said or not?"

Judah played with a strand of her hair, rubbing it between his fingers. "Yeah, we'll take Jac to the doctor, and fair warning, I've pretty much already decided to take DJ up on her offer to loan me her apartment. I'm just hoping that you cook."

Nice try, mister. "I'll cook every second night. And you'll share the responsibilities of looking after Jac, I'm not doing it by myself. I'll draw up a schedule."

"Of course, you will," Judah said, his thumb gliding over her full bottom lip. "Tell me, do you schedule sex?"

Darby jerked back, shocked. "What?"

Judah flashed her what she was coming to recognize as his pirate grin. It was cheeky and cocky and so damn in-your-face confident. He lifted one broad shoulder in an insouciant shrug. "I just thought that a woman intent on taking over the world should have a measure of stress relief."

"Not with you!" Darby said, annoyed beyond belief.

The pirate morphed back into the professional and his eyes cooled. "Obviously, not with me. We can't possibly confuse this situation with something sexual."

Her brain knew that was the sensible course of action. But her long-neglected libido vehemently disagreed.

And when she looked in Judah's blue eyes and saw the deep regret in all that blue, she suspected his libido disagreed, too.

After another shower—the quick one she had in Judah's hotel room didn't really count—Darby walked into the massive family kitchen in her house and headed straight for the coffee machine.

Needing a break, she reached for her favorite cup and shoved it under the spout of Levi's fancy coffee machine. She hit the correct button, then gripped the counter and straightened her arms, looking down at the black-and-white tiled floor beneath her flat-soled leather boots.

She needed five minutes, ten, enough time for caffeine to jolt her awake.

After returning from the doctor—her suspicions about Jac having an ear infection turned out to be correct—she and Judah hit the mall. When she suggested they stop to pick up a couple of items for Jac—more diapers and formula, clothes better suited for Boston in a blizzard—instead of hitting a discount supermarket, Judah steered his luxury SUV into the parking lot of an exclusive mall housing one of the city's most famous boutique baby stores.

By the time they left, they had not only a car seat, but also a six-foot-tall brown bear and everything in between, including baby monitors and a cot that turned into a bed suitable for a toddler. The total at the checkout had been staggering, but Judah just handed over a black credit card and didn't blink.

Judah would probably have all this stuff shipped to his apartment in New York when he was done in Boston… Did that mean he planned on seeing more of Jac?

Darby really hoped she wasn't in lust with a guy

who'd only pay attention to his daughter if and when it suited him.

Darby heard the kitchen door open and close and then the familiar sound of Levi kicking off his boots. Turning around, she watched her big brawny brother walk into the kitchen, a scowl on his face. Darby had given up trying to work out whether he was pissed at her or not; it could go either way with Levi.

They'd never been close, even though they still shared the same house, and she knew she would never have the same kind of relationship Levi shared with Jules or with DJ. He adored them. Her? Not so much.

"Hi," Darby said, her tone wary. "You're home early."

Levi pushed a hand through his dark brown hair, tinged with red. A blonde, a brunette and a redhead—none of the Brogan siblings looked alike.

"I'm heading out of town," Levi curtly replied. "I got a message from DJ saying she's loaned her apartment to Judah Huntley?"

"Yeah. He's there now." Darby pulled her cup from under the spout and automatically handed it over to her brother. She placed another cup under the spout for herself. "He's got his daughter with him, she's nine months old. I'm working with him, helping him with a project here in Boston. I've also agreed to help him look after Jac."

As she expected, disapproval settled on Levi's

masculine features. He rubbed his hand over his face.
"God, you and babies."

"What is *that* supposed to mean?"

Levi sipped his coffee and raised one powerful
shoulder. "Why do I have to hear about your latest
IVF news from Mom?"

Dammit. Darby wrinkled her nose, silently admit-
ting that she should've told him. But she'd been trying to avoid an argument, trying to avoid being told
what to do. Levi loved telling all of them what to do.
Darby hadn't listened since she was seven years old.

"Is this a good idea, Darby? Have you thought it
through?" Levi demanded.

For God's sake! She hadn't done anything but
think.

Darby, because sarcasm was her default setting
around Levi, rolled her eyes. "I'm not going to spend
tens of thousands of dollars on something I'm not
sure of, Levi! For God's sake, give me some credit!"

"Darby—"

Tired and stressed, Darby tapped her stomach.
"My body, my decision, my life. I haven't, nor will I,
ask you for cash or to help me look after my baby, if
and when I decide to have one. You don't have a say."

Darby thought she saw hurt flash in his eyes.

Then Levi surprised her by rubbing his hands
over his face. "And maybe that hurts, too, Darby,
that you can't ask me. You'll ask Mom or Jules or
DJ for help, but me? Not a damn word."

Oh, God. He was hurting. She had no idea what

to say so she just stared at him. She and Levi sniped at each other, traded insults, stuck to neutral topics. They didn't discuss anything deep; they never had.

Levi banged his coffee cup onto the kitchen table and his gaze slammed into hers. "Where did we go so wrong, Darby? Why does every conversation have to end in a fight? I just want you to be happy, to protect you! Is that so hard to understand?"

Yeah, it really was, because since she was seven years old, she'd always felt like the spare sister, the one who really didn't matter.

She opened her mouth to say...what? She had no idea.

Levi didn't give her the chance to respond. He did what he always did when they argued. He simply walked away.

In the apartment over the four-car garage, Judah stood back and looked around the room, the once perfectly decorated loft apartment now covered in bags holding baby stuff. Lots and lots of clothes and diapers and equipment and toys and...

God, babies needed a lot of things.

But he might, as Darby had suggested a few times, have gotten a bit carried away... Shoving his hands into his pockets, Judah looked down at the little girl asleep in her bouncy chair, her long lashes smudges on her cheeks, that perfect rosebud mouth slightly pursed. His heart stuttered.

Judah reminded himself that while this was a

Kodak moment, he knew better than to be affected by the pretty picture she made. This was one of those moments life gave you to lure you into thinking raising kids wasn't that tough, that it wasn't as demanding as everyone said.

It was. No question about it.

Jac was a novelty, a cute distraction, but Judah knew that after a week or two of doing the same mind-numbing, repetitive tasks, boredom would kick in. Make bottles of formula, change the diaper, pray the kid went to sleep, rinse, repeat—for weeks on end. Interrupted sleep got old very quickly and being at the beck and call of a tiny infant and then a demanding toddler who couldn't regulate her emotions or behavior was soul-numbingly, brain-meltingly boring.

He'd done it and was still convinced that having kids wasn't an option for him. Being childless left a million doors open to him: it allowed him to live out of his suitcase doing projects all over the world. If he didn't want to return to New York City, he didn't have to. He could take a holiday in Prague or Patagonia if he felt the urge. Being childless meant eating out every night, watching midnight movies, attending the opening of new art galleries, clubs and restaurants.

Having kids meant saying goodbye to fun and freedom.

He'd had neither as a teenager, and he was damned if he'd lose out as an adult. Loving and raising a child—and committing himself to a relationship—

meant sacrificing his career and his freedom. He couldn't do that. He wouldn't.

He'd give his niece, and by extension Carla, two weeks. But not a minute more.

The door to the apartment opened and Darby slipped inside, quickly closing the door to keep out the winter wind.

The slick expensive business clothes and subtle makeup were gone. Dressed up, she looked like what he knew she was, a strong independent woman in control of her life. But wearing just jeans and a simple shirt, well-worn boots on her feet and her hair pulled back into a rough ponytail, she looked younger, softer, incredibly feminine. Flat stomach, long legs, an ass that was a perfect fit for his hands. His new employee was hotter than Abu Dhabi on a scorching summer's day.

He wanted her.

He really didn't want to want her. He didn't need that much trouble in his life.

So Judah pulled his brain out of the bedroom and noticed the emotion in her eyes that hadn't been there earlier. A little pain, some confusion, too much stress. He shouldn't be curious, but he was… She was that intriguing, that compelling.

"Everything okay?" he asked.

Her smile came too quickly, was a shade too bright. "Sure, just tired."

She lied really well but he wasn't fooled. She was more than just tired. Judah watched as Darby covered Jac's new crib mattress with a sheet and stood back. Judah smiled when she picked up the teddy bear and moved it a fraction to the right. Obsessive but so damn efficient.

Jac let out a little squeak and they both whipped around, expecting to see the little girl awake. Jac's eyes fluttered open, the lips of her rosebud mouth lifted into a tiny smile before she turned her head and slid back to sleep.

"She's been asleep for a while now, do you think she's okay?" he said. "Do you think they gave her too much pain medication?"

He heard the worry in his voice and knew Darby wouldn't miss it. She lifted her hand and rubbed his shoulder. "She's fine, Judah. She didn't sleep well last night, and now that she's pain-free, she's catching up." Darby looked at her watch. "I'm going to leave her to sleep for as long as possible, but we do have to wake her up in a few hours to give her antibiotics."

"And she should be fine in a day or two?"

"She'll be fine in a couple of hours," Darby told him. "Babies usually respond quickly to medicine. Stop worrying, Daddy."

Daddy? Judah frowned, turning the word over in his mind.

He sent her a hard stare and Darby responded by lifting one thin, arched brow. "Problem?"

Well, if she still thought Jac was his, then they did have a very big problem.

Judah held up his hand. "Just give me a second."

Darby shrugged, reached for another packet and pulled out warm winter vests and leggings. Removing the tags, she placed the clothes in a laundry basket that held the soft towels and blankets they'd purchased.

Darby still believed he was Jac's dad? How was that even possible? Judah thought back over the past thirty-six hours and suddenly realized that he'd allowed Darby's original assumption to stand.

After rubbing his hands over his face, he placed his hands on his hips and stared at the floor. He'd been super reluctant to care for Jac, unwilling to play Carla's games because he wasn't the baby's father, but when he looked at the situation through Darby's eyes, he came across as an asshat of the highest order.

He lifted his head and stared at her stunning profile. "Darby."

Darby looked at him, a tiny frown creasing her smooth forehead. She had the most gorgeous skin, soft and smooth.

"Darby, I've just realized that you have the wrong end of a very large stick."

"I do?"

"Yeah. Jac isn't my daughter," Judah told her and waited for the words to penetrate.

Darby looked from him to Jac and back again. "I know you would like her not to be, but she looks just like you," she quietly responded.

Judah allowed himself a small smile at her diplomacy. "She looks just like my half brother, who looks just like me."

Darby opened her mouth, snapped it closed and opened it again. Swallowing, she held up her finger. This time it was her asking for a minute. Judah was happy to give it to her, God knew he wasn't eager to discuss the details of his brother's affair with Judah's girlfriend.

"Well, that explains a hell of a lot."

Was that really relief he heard in her voice, a little more respect? He met her eyes and saw those emotions crossing her face. He had to force his wobbly knees to lock.

Why, on such short acquaintance, did her opinion matter so much? But the relief he felt at having that faint veil of censure removed was more than he'd expected, deeper than he'd imagined.

Now for the inquisition, the long list of questions. He owed her some answers since he'd been an idiot not to realize she was acting on bad information.

Darby surprised him by placing the back of her fingers on Jac's forehead, then her cheeks. "She hasn't developed a temperature, so I think we caught the infection before it got out of control."

They were talking about Jac and her ear infection again. Thank God. He'd take the change of subject.

Judah rubbed the back of his neck. "I feel sick wondering how long she's been in pain." He sat down on the couch and placed his ankle on his knee. "Carla isn't the most attentive mother, I doubt she would've noticed, but you did, straightaway. Thank you."

"Years of babysitting." Darby rolled a tiny pair of socks together.

He shuddered. "By choice?"

She smiled at his horror. "Well, no one held a gun to my head and made me do it."

No guns had been involved in his house, but coercion, expectation and bullying had been powerful weapons. "Didn't you want to do what normal teenagers did? Dating, partying, sports?"

"Why do you assume that I didn't do those things, too? I did, I just looked after babies in between."

Oh, *balance*. Not a concept his father and stepmom were familiar with.

Darby sat down in the chair across from him and faced him. "I'm not going to pepper you with questions about Carla and your brother, so relax. But I do just want to say one thing—"

Judah braced himself for her words, told himself not to react.

"In light of what you've just told me, I deeply respect you taking Jac and looking after her."

Okay… Not what he'd been expecting. But he couldn't accept her praise.

"What else could I do, Darby? Her mom is in the hospital, my brother is God-knows-where, Jake's parents—" they'd disowned Judah, so he wouldn't call them his parents "—are useless and I couldn't let her go into foster care." He raked his fingers through his hair. "Yeah, having a baby is disrupting but she's nine months old, none of this is her fault. I will do what I need to do for a couple of weeks. It's not a life sentence."

A small smile touched Darby's sexy mouth. "And you aren't planning to become emotionally attached to her?"

He wasn't prepared to become emotionally attached to anyone. Besides, how attached could you become to someone in a few short weeks? "That's the plan."

Her amazing smile reached her eyes. "Let me know how that works out for you."

"I don't allow attachments, Darby." He wasn't sure whom he was reminding, her or himself. "It's not what I do."

She didn't break eye contact, didn't squirm or fidget. She just looked at him with eyes the color of soft rain clouds. She opened her mouth to speak, closed her eyes and shook her head. When she looked at him again, she wore a back-to-business expression.

"Jac's asleep and should sleep for a little while yet. We have the baby monitors working. Would you like to look at the study, see where we'll work?"

"No. I want to take you to bed. Any thoughts on that?" The words flew out of his mouth before he could stop them and while he wanted to regret them, he couldn't.

* * *

Darby stared at him, a little shocked, a lot turned on.

She had thoughts. Lots and lots of thoughts. Some scary. But most were variations of the phrases *yes, please* and *take me now.*

Darby watched as Judah walked over to her and placed his hands on the arms of her chair, bending his head so she could taste his sweet breath, watch desire flicker in his eyes.

He had a small scar on the underside of his chin and his tanned neck was a perfect contrast to his white shirt. Smooth warm skin to explore, thick hair to shove her fingers into, a mouth to lose herself in.

He could be her last act of madness before she headed toward single motherhood. Before she put herself on this journey that was all hope, potential heartbreak and hormones. Before she became someone's mother, she could be Darby.

Judah could be her last chance to experience desire, to lose herself in lust.

It had been so long, and she was so out of practice but since she was a woman who didn't club or bar-hop, didn't socialize that much outside of time with her family, she hadn't had many chances to meet a guy she felt attracted to and comfortable enough to give her body to. Judah might be her last hope for good sex for a long, long time.

Despite not knowing him for very long, she knew she'd be safe with him. Judging by that kiss, he'd be a considerate lover. She'd be safe in his hands. She was almost thirty, a strong, empowered woman who wasn't afraid to express her sexuality. She could do this; she *should* do this.

Yeah...*nope.*

He was too much. It was too soon. The attraction between them was too intense, too out of control. He would be like riding a wild horse, exciting but uncontrollable.

Darby forced herself to stand up, to brush nonexistent lint off her jeans. "My only thoughts are that we should get to work. We've got a lot to do."

Judah's smile was both gentle and determined. "We're going to have to deal with this chemistry at some point, Darby."

Probably. But only when she felt like she could contain the resulting explosion.

Seven

After two days of dealing with urgent business in New York, Judah ran up the stairs to the Georgian-inspired house in Boston. Before he could reach the top step, Darby opened the door and Judah allowed his eyes to skim over her, his excited heart settling and sighing. He was...

God, he'd almost said *home*.

He was back. That would do.

Jac, from her seat on Darby's hip, handed him a gummy drooling smile and waved her arms in the air. She leaned toward him and Judah felt a rush of unexpected pleasure at her gesture, idly wishing that Darby would fall into his arms as easily.

"Hey, mouse," Judah murmured, taking Jac and brushing his chin across her downy head. He'd missed her and that surprised him. He'd been reluctant to leave Jac, but Darby assured him that she could handle two nights on her own with the baby, that Darby's mother would help if Darby needed her to. He'd left, thinking he'd be so swamped in New York that he wouldn't have time to think about Jac or Darby. He'd also thought he'd welcome being diaper- and drool-free.

The opposite had happened.

He'd been in the middle of a presentation and seen a pigeon fly past the conference room's window. He'd thought of Jac and her laughter every time she saw a bird. Or a dog. A cat. A butterfly.

He'd been talking about floor space and eco-efficiency when the image of Darby bent over a desk, her nose wrinkling in concentration, flashed on the big screen of his mind. Long legs, blond hair, sexy as hell.

His concentration had taken a beating.

"I was about to take Jac for a run, she loves it." Darby gestured to the three-wheeled stroller. "How was New York?"

"Good. Busy."

Darby lifted her arms, gathered all that silky hair and pulled it into a rough ponytail, raking the strands back with her fingers. She pulled a band from her wrist and Judah watched her chest rise, her small nipples puckering in the cold wind blowing through the open door. He felt the movement in his pants and sighed.

He'd had a proposal for no-strings sex in New

York, but he'd declined. He wanted sex, but the only person he could imagine in his bed was Darby.

And she was the one person he absolutely couldn't have. Because if something went wrong, he'd not only lose the services of a fantastic architect who was anything but an intern, but also the person sharing the looking-after-Jac load.

Sleeping with Darby would be a stupid thing to do, but the more he tried not to think about it, the more he *did*. Now wanting her was becoming pretty much all consuming…

Great.

"Blow off your run and let's go for breakfast. It's Saturday, the sun is finally shining and we are on schedule, so we can take the day," Judah suggested.

He'd just got home, and he hadn't seen her for days. If she went for a run, he might not see her again for hours.

Darby walked onto the porch and headed for the enclosed back corner. The sun was weak there, but in this corner they were out of the wind and it was almost pleasant. She shook her head. "Why don't you phone the club, hire a sitter for an hour to look after Jac and come with me?" Humor danced in her eyes. "If you can keep up…"

Judah sat down on the porch swing and placed Jac on his knee. He sent Darby a steady look. "Put that competitive streak away, Brogan. Besides, we both know that in any race I'd whip your ass."

The I-can-take-you spark in her eyes morphed

into ten-foot-high flames. "Want to test that theory? I bet you'd spend the whole time eating my dust."

"The only reason I'd be behind you was to watch your spectacular ass."

Desire jumped into her eyes, softened her mouth, made her nipples tighten. He was about to stand, to pull her in for a kiss, when the door behind them opened.

Cursing, Judah watched Levi Brogan step onto the porch. He frowned at Judah and darted an enigmatic glance at Darby. "Judah, this is my brother, Levi. Levi, Judah Huntley. I'm working with him on the Grantham-Ford commission."

Judah shook Levi's hand and did an internal eye roll when Levi squeezed his hand harder than necessary. It was a mess-with-my-sister-and-I'll-mess-you-up squeeze.

Yeah, he got it.

Then Levi surprised Judah by dropping to his haunches in front of Jac. He slowly smiled and Jac waved her hands in the air, her little body quivering with excitement. Little Jac was a flirt, Judah conceded with a wry smile.

"Hey there, cutie." Levi rumbled the words, poking the tip of a gentle finger into her thigh. Jac leaned toward him and Judah allowed Levi to pick her up. Levi put Jac on his hip and picked up Jac's hand and pretended to eat her fingers. Jac howled with laughter.

Levi turned to Darby and placed his free hand

on his hip. "I'm going away for a few days. Are you going to be okay?"

"I always am, Levi."

"I'm just checking, Darby," Levi snapped, and Judah heard the frustration in his voice.

"I'm a big girl, Levi," Darby replied, steel in hers.

Levi handed Jac back to Judah and he thought he saw a flash of hurt and disappointment cross Levi's face, but it was gone so quickly he might've imagined it. The tension between the siblings was palpable and Judah suspected they'd spent most of their lives butting heads.

After a quick goodbye, Levi jogged toward and then down the stairs. Judah watched him walk over to his muscle car parked next to the detached garage. Within minutes, the low roar and hard rumble split the morning air and Judah sighed. He needed to get himself one of those…

But he didn't have a garage to house a car or time to enjoy one. His primary modes of transport were planes and hired cars and, when he needed a vehicle of his own, rentals. Judah looked at Darby and her eyes were on her brother's disappearing back.

"Complicated relationship?" he asked.

"Very." Darby sat down on the bench swing and pulled her knees up to her chest.

He shouldn't ask but he was curious, and she looked like she could do with a friend. "What happened?"

Darby was suddenly fascinated by the multicolored laces on her sneakers.

He needed to know what was going on behind that distant expression. Jac, he noticed, had fallen asleep on his shoulder. He thought about moving her to her stroller or taking her inside but shrugged the thought away. He knew to let sleeping babies lie.

"Tell me what happened, Darby."

"Why?" Darby demanded.

Always challenging, always demanding. God, she was hard work, but Judah was coming to think he might like sparring with her. Up until this point, the women in his life had been, with the exception of Carla, undemanding and acquiescent.

Darby was anything but.

"Because I asked you," Judah replied, patient. The sun was shining, Jac was asleep and he had nowhere urgent he needed to be except here, getting to know what made this fascinating, and exasperating, woman tick.

"It's not a big deal, Judah."

"Then you shouldn't have any problem telling me."

"God, you're annoying."

"So I've heard. Now stop stalling and spill."

"It's an open secret in our family that Jules is Levi's favorite sister, followed by DJ. I come a distant third."

"Why do you feel that way?"

Darby tucked her leg under her bottom and rested

the side of her head against the back cushion of the swing. She played with the edge of her long-sleeved shirt, rubbing the fabric between her thumb and index finger.

"I was seven and it was Christmas. We were open-ing presents under the tree. Levi gave Jules a music box. When you opened it, a ballerina started danc-ing and music played. It was beautiful. I loved that damn box."

"What did he give you?"

"A baseball card. It was secondhand, he didn't even bother to wrap it. He had a stack of them. I bet he just grabbed the oldest, yuckiest one and handed it over."

Judah remembered having a stack of baseball cards himself and knew that sometimes the oldest cards were the most valuable. "Who was the player?"

"It was over twenty years ago, Judah, I have no idea. I just remember throwing the card in the fire, screaming that he didn't love me, that Jules was his favorite, that he'd ruined Christmas for me. I refused to come down for Christmas lunch and cried for the rest of the day. I pretty much spoiled Christmas for everyone that year," Darby said, subdued. "Since then there's been this barrier between us. Levi and Jules have always been closer, and I've always felt like I am on the outside looking in, that he loves her far more than he does me."

"I'm sure that's not true."

"I've always been competitive, Judah, but that

Christmas was a turning point for me. From then on, every time I came in second, I've felt unloved, shortchanged, inadequate."

Judah placed his hand on Darby's slim thigh and squeezed, astounded that this remarkable, talented and intelligent woman could feel this way. She had everything going for her except the belief that she was perfectly acceptable just the way she was. Would she ever learn that she didn't need to compete with anyone?

Probably not, he conceded. And it was not—repeat, not—his job to tell her that, to show her that.

Darby sighed, and her hand dropped to rest on his. Her fingers slid between his and pleasure rocketed up his arm and down his spine, lodging in his balls.

Yep, he was hard. Though, really, when wasn't he when he was around her?

Darby dropped her head to rest her temple against his shoulder and he felt her sigh. He could imagine her soft breath on his skin, her warm lips branding him, those elegant hands skimming his skin.

God, he wanted her.

He wanted to know her, slide into her, make her his. Because she wasn't the type of girl he could have sex with and then leave, he'd have to settle for her head on his shoulder.

And that, in this moment, was almost enough.

"I just feel like Levi can't be bothered with me. But that could be my fault because my default re-action is to push him away, to tell him I don't need him." Darby sat up and linked her hands between her knees. "I need him to be my brother, not my bossy protector."

As a big brother, Judah knew what it was like trying to protect someone who didn't want his protection, who refused to listen. Darby, he suspected, was as hardheaded as Jake. Because Judah was a take-charge-and-fix-things type of guy, as he suspected Levi was, the inability to fix what was broken drove him nuts. That was why, when he reached the end of his rope with Jake, he'd had to cut his brother out of his life.

He didn't think Darby and Levi were there yet. He doubted they ever would be.

"His emotional distance hurts, Judah," Darby quietly admitted.

"Then tell him that, Darby," Judah suggested. "Men are simple creatures, we need clear direction. We don't do subtlety."

"As a species, you men are pains in the ass."

He couldn't argue with that. "Talk to your brother, Darby. You're not seven anymore, have an adult conversation with him. Tell him that you are disappointed in him, that you don't feel supported."

"Wouldn't that make me look weak?"

God, so vulnerable but so damn feisty. "He's your brother, Brogan! You're allowed to look weak with him."

Darby turned to face Judah. Looking into her spectacular eyes, his breath caught in his throat.

He had to touch her. He couldn't wait a moment longer.

Judah stood up and walked over to the stroller, placed Jac on her side and pulled a blanket up and over her shoulders. Opening the front door, he pushed Jac into the hall, hoping that the connection, the band of attraction that arced between him and Darby, would make her follow him inside.

When she closed the door behind her, he looked from her to the imposing staircase that dominated the hall and back to her flushed face.

He could see it. She wanted him as much as he wanted her.

Thank God.

Judah didn't hesitate. He took a couple of quick strides and pressed his mouth against hers.

He felt her fingertips dig into his chest. He thought she might push him away, in spite of what he'd seen in her eyes, but then her amazing lips softened beneath his and her tongue darted past his teeth, wanting to play.

Judah placed his hands on Darby's hips and lifted her up and into him, pressing his hardness into her tight stomach. Her hands snaked up his chest and then her fingers were in his hair and her tongue was tangling with his and Judah felt like he was walking on an electrified tightrope.

Time stopped, the earth stopped turning and gravity disappeared...

All because Darby was kissing him, making desperate sounds in the back of her throat. Because her hand was on his jaw, on his neck, burrowing into the collar of his shirt…

Because she wanted him.

Judah pushed his hand under her thermal exercise top and pulled it up her torso. He wanted to look down and see her creamy skin but couldn't bear the thought of pulling his mouth off hers, not yet. Maybe not ever. Pushing the fabric up, his hands passed over her breasts and his erection hardened in response to the pointy little buds.

He needed her naked, now.

Judah had to break contact with Darby's lips to pull her shirt over her head and he took the opportunity to look down.

She was as beautiful as he'd imagined. Soft skin, strong shoulders, slim but powerful. He ran a finger over her collarbone, down that creamy skin to where her nipples hardened beneath the cotton of her sports bra. That serviceable garment had to go. He wanted the gorgeousness underneath, the fury and fire, her heat.

"Judah…"

His name was a whisper and a plea. He pulled his gaze to her face. He saw trepidation, masking the desire.

Hell, no, he wanted her mindless with pleasure, squirming and panting his name, no doubt allowed.

Judah held her jaw with his hand, keeping his touch gentle. "This has nothing to do with anyone or anything but us. It's not about Jac, the commission, our work. It's just us. Only us. Only this. Tell me you understand that, Darby," he added, hearing the desperation in his voice.

Darby nodded. He said a quick prayer of thanks, ran his hand up her rib cage and his thumb swiped her nipple. He heard her intake of breath, watched her eyes cloud over. She'd stepped out of her head. Her body—her wants and needs—were calling the shots. It made him feel powerful, masculine, that he could make her agile brain stop thinking, stop running scenarios, counting the odds.

He felt like Atlas and Bogart and Clooney rolled into one. She made him weak, but he'd never felt stronger in his life.

Judah lifted her sports bra up and over her breasts and ducked his head to tug a pretty raspberry-hued nipple into his mouth. Like the juiciest fruit, her taste was a tiny burst of flavor on his tongue. Needing more, his other hand pushed between the fabric of her exercise pants to cup her butt, pushing his fingers deeper until he could feel her heat, her wet warmth.

He needed more. He needed all of her and now, immediately. He needed skin on skin, heat on heat.

But a part of him hesitated, also needing to keep checking. There was too much at stake to make a wrong move, to regret this later.

Judah pulled back and looked into Darby's passion-filled eyes. "Are we stopping or are we continuing?"

Darby's hand drifted over his stomach, moving

down. Her palm stroking the long length of him was an answer of sorts, but he needed her to say the words. They couldn't afford any misunderstandings.

He held her hand against him, forcing himself to concentrate. "Darby…"

"Mmm?" Her thumb rubbed his tip and he thought he'd lose it, there and then.

"Are we doing this?"

She smiled, and he felt his heart bungee jump out of his chest to grovel at her feet. Stupid thing. Her thumbnail drifted across the edge of his head and his eyes smacked the back of his skull.

He felt her fingers on his belt buckle, felt the first button of his jeans pop open, then another. He couldn't hold on much longer; if she didn't speak soon, he was going to explode, in more ways than one.

Then her hand was circling him, pumping him, priming him. "I don't know what you are doing," Darby murmured in her sun-and-sex voice, "but I'm going to play with this."

"Good enough," Judah muttered.

Before his brain completely closed down, he pulled his wallet from the back pocket of his jeans, dug out a strip of two condoms and placed them on the hall table. Trying to ignore, as best he could, her hand on his shaft, he pushed her exercise pants down her legs. Stepping away from her, he stood out of her reach, taking in the sight of her, looking flushed and pretty and totally turned on.

Kicking off his shoes and socks, he pushed his jeans and boxers down his legs, watching her eyes widen as she first caught sight of him. She licked her lips, her mouth a perfect O and he hardened further, a feat he didn't think was possible.

She stood next to a painting of a Brogan ancestor, a severe-looking lady dressed in ruffles and a long skirt, dark hair pulled back in a bun. Next to Darby, a hall table held photographs of her family, her mom and dad and siblings, friends and cousins. This was her family home and Judah knew, from this day onward, she'd never look at this room the same way.

Good.

He had no problem with her thinking about him every time she walked through that front door.

Judah, his hand touching her shoulder, trailed his fingers down her arm to link his palm with hers. He rested his forehead on hers, the hair on his chest brushing against her nipples. "I want you right now."

Darby found his lips, her mouth telling him the words he so badly needed to hear. He heard "yes," he heard "more," he heard her beg him to touch her, so he did.

His mouth found her jawline, tracked kisses down her neck and nibbled his way across her collarbone. He flicked a glance upward, saw her watching him, her mouth open, her eyes wild. She knew what she wanted, but to test her, he kissed the top of her breast, sucking her soft skin just hard enough to leave the faintest red mark.

Darby whimpered, need and pleasure combining to make the sweetest sound he'd ever heard.

He sucked one nipple while teasing the other with his fingers. He moved his hands down, flirting with that small patch of carefully groomed hair, lightly playing with her.

He smiled when he felt her legs fall apart, a silent gesture begging him for more. Judah obliged by rubbing his finger over her clit and Darby shot off the wall.

Liked that, did she? Well, there was more… A lot, lot more.

Judah dropped to his knees and lifted her right thigh so that her leg draped over his shoulder. Nuzzling into her, he inhaled her, his head swimming. Going down on a woman was a curiously intimate act for their first time together but he wanted to know every inch of her and this was a good place to start. Judging by her satisfied murmurs, Darby was as into it as he was.

He licked, he tugged, he pushed in, retreated and generally drove her crazy. When he felt she was close, he edged one finger, then two, into her slick channel, curled his fingers and tapped her inside walls, his tongue working her clit.

Heat—hers, his—surrounded them and Judah knew she was on the edge, so close. He wanted their first time to be like this. He wanted her to come on his tongue, for her to fall apart in his arms.

Darby arched her back and slapped her hands

against the wall behind her. He felt her clench around him, milking his fingers.

So responsive, he thought, as another orgasm hit her, this one bigger than the first. He kept working her until he was sure she was done, only lifting his head when he felt her body slump, when her supporting knee buckled.

Holding her hips to keep her steady—she looked like a feather might knock her over—he stood and held her face in his hands. So pretty, so damn sweet.

Judah covered her mouth with his, allowed her to taste herself, and sighed when one hand went down to cup his balls and the other encircled him in a hot grip. He patted the table next to them, picked up the condoms and removed the latex from its cover. Darby took the latex from him and rolled it down his shaft, so slowly he thought he might come if she didn't hurry the hell up.

"Wall or floor?" she whispered.

Judah smiled. "Neither. Stairs." Judah walked backward, sat down on the third step. "Straddle me," he ordered.

Darby didn't hesitate. She lowered herself on him, stroking her hot and still-wet core against him, sending a firestorm sprinting from his balls up his spine.

"Take me inside you," Judah said, lifting his hands to push her hair off her face. He needed to see her, wanted to look in her eyes as he made her come again.

His tip slid inside her, just a half inch, and he

gritted his teeth, reminding himself that he was a big guy and that she probably needed time to adjust.

"You okay?" he asked, keeping perfectly still.

"Fine. Just not sure if I'm doing this right."

She might be teasing but he couldn't think straight so he pushed the thought aside. "There is no wrong way for me to be inside you. Take as much time as you need…just hurry up, okay?" Okay, he hadn't meant to say that out loud.

Darby laughed and slid down him, only stopping when he was balls deep and mindless.

"Holy, holy, holy…"

He couldn't complete the sentence; he was so close to the edge. Reaching between them, he found her sensitive bud and rolled his fingers across her. He needed her to come, now, before he lost his mind.

Darby released a surprised mewl, closed her eyes and rocked hard. The chandelier above their head was a fire burst of stars, the hard staircase a feather bed, the hallway a boudoir. Darby was perfection and he pumped his hips once, maybe twice, and she shattered, allowing him to snap the cord of his control and follow her into that pleasure-drenched paradise.

When he could string a coherent thought together, he realized Darby was sprawled on top of him and her hair was in his mouth. A wooden step was trying to saw his back in half and his right thigh was cramping. His butt had, he was sure, carpet burns from the stair runner.

Yet he'd never felt better because he'd just had the

best sex of his life in the hallway of Darby's child-hood home. He couldn't, wouldn't regret a damn thing.

Maybe when his leg fell off from lack of blood, he'd feel a bit pissed, but other than that? He'd stay where he was as long as he could.

Eight

Judah sprinted around the corner leading to the Brogan house, enjoying the feeling of the bitingly cold air burning his lungs. Darby had left earlier that morning to do whatever she intended to do on her "personal" day and he'd given up trying to look after Jac and get some work done around half past three.

Desperate to exercise, he'd called the country club and within ten minutes he had a highly recommended babysitter on his doorstep. As he was about to leave the residence, Jac cooperated and fell asleep in the sitter's arms and Judah knew he had ninety minutes, two hours if he was lucky, to exercise. He'd immediately headed for the state-of-the-art gym at the club and followed that session with a punishing run.

Now, Judah approached Darby and Levi's house

and frowned when he saw a luxury car pulling into the driveway. Slowing down, he watched as a slim blonde woman exited the car and walked around to the passenger door. Frowning, he watched Darby slowly climb out. The older blonde, who could only be Darby's mom, placed her arm around Darby's waist as they slowly walked up the steps to the front door.

Judah released a low curse and accelerated, reaching them as they hit the top of the steps. "What's the matter? What happened?"

Mother and daughter both turned, and Judah frowned at Darby's pale, pale face. "Are you okay? Where's your car?"

Callie placed a hand on his arm. She quickly introduced herself and then said, "Darby's fine, Judah. She's had a minor procedure. She's sore. I'm driving because she isn't allowed to drive for twenty-four hours."

"Where's Jac?" Darby demanded, her mouth tight with worry.

Judah jerked his head toward the front door. "I hired a sitter from the club. She was sleeping when I left."

Callie smiled at Darby before giving her a gentle hug. "I'm going to leave you in Judah's capable hands, darling. Take it easy, okay? I'll call you in the morning."

"Wait, Mom…what?" Darby frowned as Callie all but jogged down the steps. Looking from her to Judah, Darby threw her hands up in the air. "She was going to look after me, be at my beck and call, help me with Jac."

"I'm here, so is the sitter." Judah opened the door and gestured for her to step inside the warm house. He saw her wince and her hand went to her side. Concerned by her dull eyes and pinched mouth, he didn't hesitate. He bent down and scooped her up, holding her against his chest.

"Dammit, Huntley, I can walk," Darby hissed, thumping his chest.

"It'll be quicker if I carry you."

Judah swiftly carried her down the hallway to the study, kicked the door open with his foot and gently placed her on the large sofa in front of the enormous flat-screen TV that dominated one wall. Sitting down on the coffee table in front of her, he allowed his hands to dangle between his legs, reminding himself that he couldn't interrogate her. He didn't have that right.

"Where the hell have you been and what happened?"

Not a good start. But he needed to know she was okay, that she wasn't ill or injured. He placed his hand on his heart and tried to rub away the burn. He hated to see her injured, hurt, a diluted version of the vibrant woman he knew.

Darby couldn't meet his eyes, so Judah gripped her chin to lift her face. In her eyes, he saw traces of embarrassment, a truckload of defiance and underneath it all, fear. He gentled his touch, gave her a small smile. "Darby, a million things are running through my mind right now, none of them good."

Darby sucked in air, then grimaced. "I had my eggs harvested today. It turned out to be a bit more painful than I expected."

Judah frowned. What? What on earth was she talking about? "I'm sorry, I don't understand."

Darby drew patterns on her leggings with the tip of her index finger. "I have severe fertility problems. I will never be able to conceive a child naturally and it's been recommended that if I want children, I undergo IVF within the next few months. The first step is having my eggs harvested and then frozen."

Judah opened his mouth to say something sympathetic, then abruptly pulled the words back. She didn't need sympathy, she needed understanding and he didn't know where to start with that. "And I'm presuming you want kids?"

Darby touched her top lip with the tip of her tongue. "Yes. I can't afford to wait so I'm doing this solo."

Brave, brave woman. And so Darby: there was something she wanted so she went out and grabbed it.

Judah heard the knock on the door and the sitter poked her head around. "I heard you come in. Jac's in her playpen. I gave her a bottle and a banana for a snack. I hope that's okay?"

Judah nodded. "Do you have anywhere you need to be?" he asked. "Can you hang around for another two hours?"

She nodded. "Sure."

The door closed behind her and Judah looked at Darby, worried. She looked so pale, so tired. "Can I get you something? Coffee? Cocoa? Pain pills?"

"I took some meds earlier," Darby replied. She picked up her legs to lie down on the couch. She tucked a pillow under her head. "Thanks for not making an inane comment about my wonky womb."

He knew she was trying to sound brave, but she just sounded defeated. Judah lifted his hands and spread them apart. "Honestly, Darby, I have no idea what you are feeling. I am exactly the opposite. I really don't want kids and am very happy with the idea of being childless."

"Really?"

Judah nodded. "Yeah."

"Can you tell me why?"

They were wading into uncharted territory, into deeper waters. This conversation would take them from colleagues who were sleeping together to... something deeper, undefinable. He didn't like deep or undefined, but she'd been honest with him and he needed to—wanted to—reciprocate.

Judah couldn't think of a decent reason not to tell her the truth. "My brother is twelve years younger than me and when he was born, I, somehow, ended up being his primary caregiver," Judah stated, his tone flat. "My father and stepmom's contribution to raising Jake was to make him and birth him. Up until I left for college, I all but raised him."

Darby shook her head, as if she didn't believe what he was saying. "You mean you looked after him after school, you helped him with his homework, that kind of stuff, right?"

This is why he never spoke about his childhood. People—Darby type of people—never wanted to believe what he was telling them. "No, I looked after him. He was born at the beginning of the summer holidays when I was twelve, and my stepmom had very bad postpartum depression. She literally could not take care of him and my dad had to work. When I had to go back to school, she roused herself enough to look after him until I got home but then I was on duty while she slept or went out. Somehow, God knows how, the responsibility of raising Jake was passed on to me."

"Oh, God, Judah, that's horrible."

He shrugged and noticed the empathy in her eyes. Thank God there was no pity. Pity made his skin crawl. "I didn't have time to do sports or date or do anything at all. My job was to take care of my brother. When my father started making noises about me attending a local college, I knew I had to do something to escape so I studied and got a full-ride scholarship. I abandoned Jake to save myself."

God, he hadn't meant to say that last part. There was something about Darby that made him want to open up, and that scared the crap out of him.

Darby linked her hands around her knees, her

eyes focused on his face. "And the guilt nearly killed you."

Judah lifted one shoulder in acknowledgment of her statement. "I tried to come home as often as I could but every time I came home, I felt Jake slipping further and further away from me. He was so mad at me for leaving so he did whatever he could to piss me off. Joyriding, boosting cars, alcohol, weed, stronger drugs."

"You had a right to live your life, Judah, to have a life."

He knew that, he *did*. Intellectually. "Jake's never stopped being pissed at me."

"And that's why he had an affair with your girlfriend."

Judah winced. "Yep. I loaned her my apartment in Manhattan. She had a gig at The Met and I was in Australia on a project. Jake, somehow, hooked up with her and moved in. I caught them in bed together and gave them the rest of the day to clear out. Jake took my meaning literally, he stripped my apartment. Anything that he could sell for drugs, he did."

Darby lifted her fist to her mouth, seeming shocked and pissed on his behalf. "I hope you had him arrested."

She got it, thank God. Choices and consequences… "My father insisted I drop the charges or I'd be kicked out of the family."

"You chose the latter," Darby said, her voice holding no trace of judgment.

"He served a year. I'm blamed for his criminal record. My family and I have no contact."

Darby shook her head in disbelief. "After all you did for Jake? Unbelievable."

After so long, it felt both strange and wonderful to have someone get it, to have someone smart and together and thoughtful be on his side, agreeing with his choices. The hand squeezing his lungs eased and the guilt, for the first time in years, retreated. Judah felt like he could breathe. "So that's why I don't want kids. I've been a dad, it wasn't that great."

Darby touched his hand with the tips of her fingertips. "And you've never had second thoughts?"

Judah shook his head. "No, in fact, I even came really close to having a vasectomy about a decade ago."

Darby's smile was both humorous and self-deprecating. At his lifted eyebrow, she shrugged. "I was just thinking that we are a badly matched pair. You don't want kids, I do. Thank God there's nothing more between us than great sex. We'd be disastrous together."

Apart from them disagreeing about what they wanted from life—that little thing!—they were damn good together. Sexually and mentally compatible, equally strong, equally independent. She was the only woman he'd ever encountered whom he could see in his life five or ten years down the track. That had never happened before, and he wasn't sure how to deal with her, what to think.

Judah noticed her heavy eyes, so he leaned forward and placed his lips to her forehead, keeping them there for longer than he intended. "Sleep, sweetheart. I'll be here when you wake up."

Mason rolled off Callie and stalked naked to her en suite bathroom. After cleaning up, he gripped the edges of one of the freestanding basins and stared at his reflection in the mirror above his head. He looked the same, he noted. Blue eyes, a three-day beard. Same mouth, nose, body...

So then why did he feel like he was a stranger inside his skin?

Flipping on the tap, he bent down to drink water from his hand before splashing it on his face. Four months ago, five, he was living a perfectly normal life as a single father, having discreet affairs when time and circumstances allowed. He'd been reasonably content running his coffee shop, running herd on his boys. Coasting.

Then Hurricane Callie blew into his life.

He'd thought it so damn simple: he liked her, they'd have sex, they'd keep having sex for as long as it was fun. Then they'd drift apart, no harm, no foul.

But here he was, two and a half months into the year, and he was floundering. His business was successful, but it was boring; his kids were growing more independent by the day, and living in this community was like living in a goldfish bowl. Mason was so damn jealous of Callie's trip to Thailand, of her freedom to pick up and go.

Actually, every time he thought about Thailand his brain wanted to explode.

"Let's talk, Mace."

Mason turned to see Callie standing in the doorway, her lush body covered with a white robe, holding two glasses of red wine. Walking over to her massive square cedar-clad bathtub, she sat down on the edge and crossed her legs.

She nodded to a towel and Mason grabbed it, wrapping it around his hips before taking a glass from her. He gulped and leaned his shoulder into the wall.

"It's not the same, is it?" Callie asked, her eyes wide and blue.

He wanted to lie, but he didn't. "No." But that didn't mean it was bad, just different.

"Is it because I've come out of my shell...sexually?"

Mason nearly choked on his wine. "God, no." Her sexual confidence was amazing and such a turn-on. The sex was the only thing going right at the moment.

"Then what's the problem, Mace?"

How to put this into words? He was a numbers guy; they made sense. His annoying, undefinable feelings were harder to explain.

He raked his hand through his hair. "I can't put my finger on it, but I feel like I am looking at a math problem and I know the formula is wrong, but I don't know why."

Callie nodded. "With me or with your life?"

Mason shrugged. Feeling like he was frying in the spotlight, he decided to swing it onto her. "You're different, too, Callie."

Callie tipped her head and waited for him to continue.

"You're calmer, more centered. Less nervous, more confident."

"And that's a problem?"

No…but it was different.

"Are you tired of the chase, Mason?" Callie asked in a bland tone.

Her eyes were shadowed, and he couldn't read how she was feeling, couldn't discern what she was thinking. Before the New Year, before her Southeast Asia travels, he'd been able to read her. Now she seemed like a closed book.

Then her words sank in and he felt impossibly, undeniably angry. "*What* did you ask me?"

Callie swirled her wine in her glass and refused to meet his eyes. "Months ago, I was lost, quite naive, lacking in confidence sexually. Then I ran into you, all big and bold, demanding that I face life again, that I enjoy you and sex and kissing and touching. I listened, and I took a chance on you." Callie raised her eyes to him and grimaced. "We had a marvelous week between Christmas and New Year's. The night of the party, I stepped back from you, just for a moment, and you used my actions as an excuse to run."

Her words lodged in his skin and exploded as little bubbles of truth. Not able to deal with how much he enjoyed being with her, how wonderful he'd felt having her in his life, he'd used Ray as an excuse.

Mason's feelings for her scared him and he'd run. *Ouch.*

But because he was in the wrong, he did what guys do and went on the attack. "I didn't run as far as you."

"Fair point. But I took my ring off, put Ray's photo away and, crucially, I came back. We've been together twice since the coffee shop encounter, we have had what I thought was miraculous sex but... but I feel like something is off. The only conclusion I can come to is you are tired of the chase."

He couldn't let her think that. "It's not that, Cal. I'm not tired of you."

"Well, I'm not going to sit here and play guessing games with you, Mace." Callie stood up and folded her arms across her chest, her wineglass resting against her upper arm. "I'm going to be the adult and tell you what I am feeling, dealing with. I'm not ready to slide into retirement, to live the rest of my life as a wealthy widow. I want to do something, Mason, be someone. I've always been Ray's wife or the kids' mom, supporting their dreams, their goals, their interests. I want to *contribute.*"

He loved her fire, her determination to keep growing as a person and carve out her place in the sun.

Oh, God, he thought he might love her.

"I've been looking into some projects I can contribute to, but you should know that I'm not going to be living here on an ongoing basis. I loved traveling, Mason, I want to do more of it. I loved Bali and Thailand and there are so many more places I want to see, experience." Callie pulled in a deep breath and tried to smile. "I'm crazy about you, Mace, but if I stay here, content to coast, to wait for visits from you, I'll find myself drifting again and then I'll be lost. I don't want to be lost again."

Mason, touched beyond belief, had no words. He feared losing her, but he was even more terrified of asking her to stay, asking her to sacrifice herself to be with him. He valued freedom—his own and others'—too much do that to someone he adored.

Instead of talking, he pulled her into his arms and tucked her head under his chin. He understood her need to fly, he just needed to find a way to hand her a set of wings.

Or to find a set of his own.

Darby walked into the games room at the Brogan house and quickly scanned the area.

Judah, Noah, Matt and Levi were playing a game of pool on the table first bought by a Brogan ancestor at the turn of the century. A barrage of insults flew across the green fabric and Darby winced; four alpha men, it was bound to get competitive. Good thing she wasn't playing.

She walked over to the table and saw that Judah had a difficult shot to make.

"You're a decent player, Judah. You should play Darby sometime. She likes to play, and we don't like playing with her."

Judah fell into Noah's trap. "She's that bad, huh?" he said, looking up from his bent position over the table.

Darby forced a scowl onto her face. "Hey! I'm not *that* bad."

"We hate playing you, Darby," Matt said, whistling as Judah made the trick shot.

Huh, Judah might be worth her time. She could challenge him to a game of strip pool. It would be fun to see how quickly she got him out of his clothes.

Judah walked around the table, patted her butt and dropped a sexy "yes" in her ear.

Darby rolled her eyes. "Yes to what?"

"Yes, to whatever you're cooking up regarding you and me and pool," Judah whispered, pulling her hair away from her neck to place his lips beneath her ear. Unconcerned by their amused audience, he pressed his big body against her back, his hand on her stomach, and he felt so warm, smelled so amazing. And that mouth on her sensitive skin…dynamite.

"And why," Judah growled, his voice back to its normal level, "do I have this sneaky suspicion these guys are trying to hustle me? I think you might be good at pool. Good as in exceptional."

Darby tried to keep her face innocent as she turned around. "Why would you think that?"

Darby melted under his sexy grin, aware that the game was over and that her friends had moved on to discussing a new yacht Matt was designing. "Their very careful choice of words. They do hate playing with you because you are good. That's not a surprise because there isn't a damn thing you aren't good at and you're competitive. And I'm not an idiot."

Dammit. Judah had a hell of brain to go with that gorgeous face and brawny body.

"And yes, strip pool would be fun," he quietly added.

Darby threw up her hands, laughed at his smirking expression and turned her back on their game. Needing to get some distance before she embarrassed herself by throwing her arms around Judah and kissing him comatose, Darby walked over to the fireplace. DJ and Jules sat on the squishy couch and Callie sat opposite them, totally absorbed by the baby sitting in her lap.

Mason wasn't here at this family dinner and that was a surprise.

DJ looked up and smiled. "Oh, Lordy, Darby, you have to hear the latest nonsense Mrs. Jenkins has come up with. I swear the old lady is losing her mind."

Mrs. Jenkins had been ancient when they were

kids. For as long as they could remember, in rain or snow or hailstorms, every afternoon she hopped on her motorized scooter and did a tour of the grounds. She was the community's primary source of news and gossip.

"She said she saw a half-naked woman in the window of Mason's coffee shop last Wednesday. She was plastered up against the glass door and a man was kissing her."

Yeah, the sweet old thing was losing it. Mason would never let something like that happen at his place. Darby thought back. "Last Wednesday was the height of the blizzard, no one was out."

"I think she's getting a little more senile," Callie said, her hands over her face as she played peeka-boo with Jac, who thought it was a brilliant game.

"Has Mason said anything about the rumor, Mom?" Jules asked.

"Mason doesn't listen to rumors. But I'm sure he'll find the story amusing," Callie said. Holding on to Jac, she stood up, her cheeks tinged with pink. "Uh, it's getting a bit hot this close to the fire."

Darby, who was standing closer, hadn't noticed the heat. "I think it's you, Mom."

Callie flushed a deeper red. "Me? What's me?"

Why was her mom acting so weird? "Are you getting sick? Do you have a temperature? There's a lot of flu going around."

Callie nodded. "I'm fine, don't fuss. Come on, Jac, let's go change you."

Darby looked at Callie's departing back. She'd changed Jac not a half hour ago but…okay. Since returning from Bali, her mom had been acting a little weird.

Turning back to her twin and best friend, Darby remembered something she'd been wanting to ask. "Listen, have either of you two borrowed my thigh-high black boots, the sexy ones I bought for that Halloween party? I can't find them anywhere."

Jules and DJ said they didn't think so, but they would check—their closets were a mess of borrowed items—and the conversation moved on. Darby, curled up in the opposite sofa, tuned out and just watched her family.

In all her dreams growing up, this is what she'd imagined. Her sisters, one by blood, the other by heart, were happy and in love with good men, her mom was seeing a man who wasn't her dad and she was okay with that. And there was a man across the room who made her feel amazing every single day. Jac was as sweet as sugar and wonderfully easy to look after.

Her business was going well. She was a professional success and she should be happy.

Except that she wasn't. It was all a lie, a sham, an illusion. Oh, not her sisters, they were, as far as she knew, as happy as they looked, and her mom seemed reasonably content, but as for the rest? The baby, the man?

Darby and Judah weren't what they looked like.

Darby closed her eyes against the familiar wave of pain and embraced it, allowing the barbs and the spurs to pick at her skin. She welcomed the way it scratched and burned because pain was better than fooling herself, imagining there was a chance this was what the rest of her life would look like. There was no possible way it could.

No matter how she looked at it, a happy-ever-after was not possible for her and Judah.

Their relationship was tied into this short-term project and into looking after Jac. The little pretend family they'd so swiftly become had an imminent expiration date. The news from Italy was good, Carla was recovering nicely and was interviewing nannies. They were expecting the call that would whip Jac out of their lives.

Darby, as the local liaison for Huntley and Associates, had everything for the museum project under control, and she knew Judah had a bid on a project in Kuala Lumpur and he'd been approached to design an eco-friendly lodge in Costa Rica.

He'd hand Jac back to Carla, kiss the baby goodbye and move on with his life. And Darby should look to move on with hers. She had to make a definite decision about whether to try IVF.

No matter what happened in the future, she was glad she'd had this time with Jac; it had given her a realistic idea of what caring for a baby day in and day out meant. She had a better idea of the work involved, how much energy it took. If she had to do it on her own, she could but...

But it would be so much easier with a partner, with Judah.

But Judah didn't want kids.

Ever.

And she'd, foolishly, fallen in love with him. Dammit. Her heart was convinced he was her forever man, but her brain couldn't fathom how she could love someone who didn't want what she wanted. How could he be so fabulous with Jac—patient, kind, calm—but not want to experience having a child himself? How had that happened? Why had it happened? How could life be this cruel?

Darby rested her head against the cool column, reluctantly respecting his decision not to procreate but also not understanding it. Judah was warm, funny, loving... In her opinion, he should have kids. He needed a partner, a home, children.

Over the past week they'd discussed her desire to have a child, his desire to remain childless, and she knew there was no hope of a future with him that looked anything like the future she wanted, of a house filled with noisy boys and feisty girls.

Even if she and Judah agreed to keep seeing each other after Jac left—the distance between Boston and New York wasn't that far—Darby knew nothing would come out of it but some sexy times. Judah would never love her like Noah loved Jules, like Matt loved DJ.

Darby was competitive, she admitted it, and knowing that her lover didn't love her the same way her sister's and friend's men loved them—with everything they had—would kill her. It would be a slap in the face at every family gathering. She'd be reminded that Judah might love her body, appreciate her skill as an architect, but he still chose to stand apart from her and from everything that a family meant.

It would be better, cleaner, if they all moved on now. Jac needed to go back to Carla, Darby needed to try IVF, Judah needed to do whatever Judah wanted to do.

Darby bit her bottom lip, her eyes on Judah. He wore chinos and a loose white button-down shirt with the sleeves rolled up. He hadn't shaved for a couple of days and his stubble gave him a rakish air. He looked hot and amazing. Her life and her bed were going to be lonely, lonely places without him in it.

As if he felt her eyes on him, Judah snapped his head up and looked for her. Finally finding her, he frowned. Heading toward her, he laid his arms on the back of the sofa and touched his knuckle to her cheekbone.

"Hey, you okay?"

Darby forced a smile onto her face. "Sure. I was just about to go and find Jac. Callie took her, saying she needed to be changed."

At that moment, Callie appeared in the doorway

to the living room, Jac in her arms. "Supper is almost ready. Can I have some help in the kitchen?"

Judah's hand on Darby's shoulder kept her in place while the others obeyed Callie's cheerful request. When they were gone, Judah rested his hip on the back of the sofa. He placed his big hand on her bent knee. "What's going on, Darby? You look a little lost."

Whether it was to her work or to her body, Judah paid attention. "I just wanted a minute to think."

"I expected you to be at the pool table, telling Noah and Levi how to sink their shots," Judah teased.

"I'm not that bad."

Darby met his eyes and saw the speculation in them, knew she wasn't hitting the light tone she was aiming for. Trying to distract him, she reached for the bottle of beer in his hand. She took a long sip and rested the bottle against her cheek. "I have a slight headache."

"When are you going to realize you can't lie to me, Brogan? Something else is going on inside that big brain of yours."

"I'm fine, Judah."

"No, you're not. I've been watching you for a while and you're anything but fine," Judah persisted. He squeezed her knee. "Talk to me, Darby."

She couldn't. She couldn't tell him that she loved him, that she wanted the dream, the full house, the family dinners with kids they'd raised together.

Feeling like her skin was too tight for her body, Darby stood up. "Have you spoken to Carla lately?"

"Yeah."

"Any word on when Jac is going back?"

Judah's mouth compressed to a thin line. "Soon. Within the next few days."

Darby nodded, telling herself she would not cry. "I'm going to miss her."

"I know." Judah raked his hair back, his eyes miserable. "If I had known you wanted children so badly, I would never have asked you to look after her."

"You didn't ask, you offered me a deal. I took it."

"Still, it wasn't fair to you."

He made it sound like he'd forced her into looking after Jac. That simply wouldn't do. "I'm an adult, Judah, I make my own decisions. Looking after Jac has been fun but…" She hesitated.

"But?" Judah pressed.

Darby gathered the scattered bits of her courage. "But I'm sort of glad she's going soon. I'm getting attached and the longer she stays, the harder it's going to be to say goodbye," Darby said, keeping her voice low.

Judah didn't say anything for a long, long time. "That bad, huh?"

Yeah, it was that bad.

But she didn't want only the little girl, she wanted the man and her dream and the house and… No, enough. She had to stop thinking about what she didn't have and look forward to what she could have. Being a single mom, raising a child on her own.

She tasted panic, fought to find air. She could do it; she *would* do it.

And really, she had to let Judah go, to do his own thing. She refused to live her life hoping he'd change, that he'd come to love her enough to give her something she wanted but he didn't. Sleeping with him, staying with him, playing happy families with him was too difficult; she couldn't do it for much longer.

She loved him and every time she made love with him, she fell a little harder, a little deeper. Every time they argued about architecture, discussed books, art, sports, politics, she found herself rolling around in his mind, enjoying his sharp intellect and his dry humor.

She loved him and loving him was starting to feel a little like torture.

"What do you want, Darby?" Judah quietly asked, his expression as serious as she'd ever seen it.

He'd said that nobody could become attached in two weeks, but he'd been so wrong.

"Unfortunately, I want everything, Judah. I want it all."

Nine

Having abandoned DJ's apartment to move in to the big house the day after he and Darby first made love, Judah opened the back door to the mudroom, kicked off his boots and shrugged out of his coat. Outside, the wind was picking up and the clouds were low in the sky. The weather reporters were talking about another massive nor'easter hitting Boston sometime during the night and they would wake up to many inches of snow.

The house was quiet, and Judah frowned. For the past fifteen years, he'd treasured quiet but now it seemed oppressive, almost strange. After just two weeks, he was used to music, Jac's squeals, Darby singing off-key, a radio or television playing in the background.

The sounds of home.

Wondering where his girls were, Judah pulled out his phone to call Darby, but before he could pull up her number, his phone rang. He stared at the phone like it was an annoyed snake ready to strike, knowing the call would flip his life back to normal.

He didn't want his life to go back to how it had been. He loved his life with Darby, with Jac.

He shouldn't. But he did.

The call died, but two seconds later, the same number popped up on his screen. He couldn't avoid her. He had to have this conversation.

"Carla."

"Hello, Judah." Carla's voice sounded thin and thready. Nothing like the sultry tones he remembered so well. "How's my girl? How is Jacquetta?"

Happy. Content. Full of smiles. Judah swallowed those words and opted for a simple reply. "She's fine. Are you out of the hospital?"

"I am back at my home in Como. With a full-time nurse. Luca has hired a nanny for Jac, an American who has a degree in early childhood development."

Jac didn't need a teacher, she needed a mom.

"I need peace and quiet to recover, to build my strength. The nanny and Jac will live in the cottage until I am recovered enough to have them in the house."

Jac wasn't the noisy equivalent of a construction site. Carla had undergone an appendectomy, not a heart transplant. *God.*

"She's not an untrained puppy, Carla, she's your daughter!" Judah said. He ground his teeth together so hard he was sure he felt enamel pepper his tongue.

"Nevertheless, it's imperative that I focus on myself, in doing whatever I can to recover quickly. I will send the nanny to come and get Jacquetta. She will be there on Friday. Please have her packed and ready to go."

Over my cold, dead body.

Judah gripped the bridge of his nose so hard that a sharp pain ricocheted into his sinuses. "I am not handing Jac over to some stranger."

Carla waited a beat before speaking again. "Then the only other alternative is for you to bring her to me."

"If that's what I have to do," Judah ground out.

Carla's husky voice drifted into his ear. "Don't worry so much, Judah. The nanny is good, and I will try to be a better mother to Jacquetta."

If wishes were horses and all that crap. And her name was Jac…

"I want normality, Judah, a simple life. A man, my baby, sun on my face, fresh air and good food. Just a simple life."

Carla wouldn't know simple if it bit her on the butt. Judah raised his eyes to the ceiling and pushed his shoulder into the wall. As soon as she was better, this conversation would be forgotten, and she'd be fighting her way back into the limelight. She was the moth that needed the flame of attention and she'd burn herself, and everyone around her, before she stepped out of the fire.

Poor Jac.

Thinking about Jac constantly looking for Carla's attention lit the detonation cord attached to his explosive temper. "Try to remember that Jac is not a damned book you can loan out, have returned and loan out again, Carla. She's a little girl and she needs stability. Can you give her that?"

"Stability is overrated. I never had any as a child but I'm okay."

Okay was a nebulous term. Her okay was his very messed up.

"Bring Jacquetta home, Judah. You'll never have to be bothered with her again."

Judah heard the phone disconnect and shook his head, lifting the phone to bang it against his forehead.

Jesus, how was he going to tell Darby that Jac was leaving? How was he going to find the strength to take her back? But he had to...

Jacquetta wasn't Darby's and she sure wasn't his. He didn't want kids, remember?

He needed to go back to his old life, back to freedom, to long nights working at his desk, early morning walks through whatever city he happened to be in, or sleeping the morning away, waking up and finding a small local restaurant for a late lunch. Working through the next night...

No one to report to, no one to worry about, no one to worry about him.

So, if that was what he wanted, why did he feel hollow inside?

Annoyed with himself, Judah walked into the kitchen, tossed his phone onto the marble-topped island and padded into the hall. At the bottom of the stairs, he finally heard girly laughter. He was too far away to hear individual words, but he allowed the soft feminine sounds to wash over him. As he climbed the stairs, the words became more distinct and Darby's off-tune voice became stronger.

Judah walked down the long hallway of the first floor and wondered how he could go back to silence. How was he supposed to embrace freedom when freedom didn't include Darby's singing and Jac's bold smile and naughty laughter?

Judah pushed open the door to Darby's bedroom, sighed at the mess—an unmade bed, a lilac bra on the floor, a trail of her clothes leading to the bathroom. Judah nudged open the door to the bathroom with his shoe and looked toward the massive claw-foot bathtub in the corner.

Woman and baby were a study in contrasts, light and dark, equally compelling, stunningly beautiful. The bath was filled to the brim with both water and bubbles and Darby leaned back, knees poking out. Jac was sitting on her stomach, scooping bubbles out of the water and trying to eat them.

Darby's eyes were on the little girl, and through

her smiles, he saw, possibly for the first time, her need to have her own child, the depth of her longing.

Yeah, he knew she feared the responsibility, that she was questioning whether she was on the right path, but he saw her desire to be a mommy, how much she wanted to be the center of a child's universe. He'd understood, on an intellectual basis, why she'd had her eggs harvested, but only in this minute did he understand her soul-deep need for someone to call her Mom.

It utterly terrified him.

Yet, he wanted to give her a child, his child.

Not because he wanted to be a dad or because children were what he wanted, but because, for the first time in a long time, he valued someone else's happiness above his own. Darby wanted children, her *own* children, and he would do anything in his power to give them to her.

The thought made beads of sweat break out on his forehead. Making a baby, making babies, with Darby was a hell of a big deal. It would be the biggest project of his life.

Judah wiped the moisture from his forehead, wishing he could fully embrace the life she craved, but he couldn't imagine being fully responsible for another human or being invested in their welfare. He'd done that with Jake and looked how it had ended: Jake was a drug-addicted ex-con and Judah had no idea where his brother even was.

How he wished Darby didn't have this need to

procreate, that they could be a family of two. She was a talented architect, they worked well together, and he could see them traveling the world, designing buildings in foreign and exciting places. For the first time in his life, he could imagine settling down. He could imagine them buying a plot of land—maybe here in this community—and designing their perfect house. Jules would decorate it and they'd spend some of their time in Boston, the rest somewhere else, anywhere else.

They could be free, unencumbered.

But Darby wanted a baby and he wanted to be the guy who gave it to her.

But he knew if he did that, she would also insist he be a dad, be *the* dad. She wouldn't allow him to half-ass anything. He would have to step up to the plate.

Could he do that, be that person, for her? To make her happy?

Hell, he would do anything to make her happy… He was in love with her…maybe.

God, he didn't know what love felt like, but he thought about her all the time. He couldn't get enough of her luscious body. Making her smile and laugh was his priority. He enjoyed talking to her. She was the only person who knew about his past and the impact it had on him. Over the course of two weeks, he'd found his best friend and his lover, had met the one person who was able to crack open his withered soul, climb inside and warm it up.

He didn't want kids, but he'd have them.

For her.

With her.

Jac's delighted squeal refocused his attention on the very pretty scene in the bathtub. Jac waved her hands in welcome and Darby tipped her head back to look at him, a sexy smile on her face.

"Hey." She sat up, half turned and smiled slowly. "You look cold. And miserable."

She had no idea. He needed to tell her that Jac was leaving, that he had to take her back. When Darby reconciled herself to Jac leaving, he'd tell her that he wanted to keep seeing her, that he was prepared to father her child, her children. That he'd do this, for her.

Darby frowned, looking to the window, and Judah followed her gaze. Snow was starting to fall and if he didn't have the weight of his news on his shoulders, it would be a lovely scene. A naked Darby, snow, a big bath…

Judah glanced at his watch and realized it was Jac's bedtime. Maybe he could put off the news until tomorrow. They could heat up the water in that bath and he could draw pictures on Darby's skin with bubbles.

Darby snapped her fingers, pulling his gaze from her lovely breasts to her even lovelier face. "What's going on, Judah?"

Judah walked over to the heated towel rack, pulled off a warm fluffy towel and reached for Jac. After nuzzling her cheek, inhaling her precious baby smell, he wrapped her in the towel and cradled her against his chest.

He looked down at Darby and smiled. "I'll dress her and put her to bed."

A small frown pulled Darby's eyebrows together. "I left her bottle in a warmer on my bedside table. She should go down fast, she's exhausted."

Judah didn't reply, he just bent down to place his lips against Darby's. Through his touch, he tried to warn her, to comfort her, to reassure her that they would be okay, that he had a plan. He felt her hesitancy, her fear, and sighed against her lips.

He'd do anything not to hurt her. He'd do anything at all.

But, as much as he wanted to, he couldn't give her Jac.

Judah half closed the door of Jules's old room, allowing the light from the hallway to spill into the space where Jac was sleeping. Opening the door to Darby's bedroom, the place where they'd loved and laughed, he sat on the edge of her bed and waited for her to come out of the bathroom.

This wasn't a conversation he could have when she was naked.

Resting his forearms on his thighs, he stared down at the hardwood floor beneath his feet, conscious of a pounding headache behind his eyes. Emotional connections—this was why he'd avoided them.

"She's going back, isn't she?"

Judah looked up. Darby stood in the doorway, his sweatshirt hanging down to her thighs, her hair in a messy knot on top of her head. He immediately noticed the haunted look in her eyes, the wobbly lower lip.

He nodded. "Yeah."

Darby's arms wrapped around herself and her face paled. "When?"

"As soon as possible. I'll charter a jet in the morning and we'll leave as soon as we can." Judah flexed his fist. Apart from walking away from Jake, this was going to be the hardest thing he'd ever done.

Why had he agreed to look after her, why hadn't he insisted that Luca make another plan? Oh, because she was Judah's niece, her father was a drug-addicted loser and there had been no one else. Darby had warned him, but he hadn't thought he could become this attached, this soon. Sending Jac back was turning out to be insanely horrible for him and he knew Darby was as deeply affected.

Had he known how much she wanted children, he would never have asked her to become involved in Jac's life. But by the time he found out, he couldn't let Darby go.

He would never be able to let her go.

Judah stood up, walked over to her and skimmed his knuckle over her still-damp cheek. From her bath or from tears? He couldn't tell.

"Are you okay?"

Darby lifted one shoulder. "It's not as if we didn't know this was going to happen."

That wasn't an answer. "Carla's her mother, Darby, we can't keep her."

Darby sent him a sharp look. "I know that, Judah. I never expected to keep her, I'm not that much of a delusional idiot."

She's hurt, she's upset, be gentle. "I don't think you're an idiot. I just know you've bonded with Jac and it has to hurt to let her go." He kept his voice low and even. This situation was tough enough. He didn't want to argue.

Darby pushed past him and walked around the bed to stand at her window, moving aside the drapes to look at the swiftly falling snow. "You are acting like this is all about me, like I'm the only one who'll be affected by her leaving. You're going to miss her, too, Judah."

Sure. But there was no point in dwelling on that.

Darby whirled around, her eyes enormous in her colorless face. "I know you watch her when she sleeps, Judah. I see how affectionate you are with her, the love you have for her."

Judah rubbed the back of his neck. "She's a cute kid and she is my niece, Darby."

"She's more than that and you know it! Why won't you fight for her?" Darby demanded. "She has a useless mother, who is going to hand her off to a nanny as soon as you land. She'll have everything she'll ever want but she won't have one damn thing she needs! She won't have a parent to raise her, to teach her, to guide her."

"So, you think I should just demand that Carla hand over custody to me?" Judah raised his voice. Was she nuts? That wasn't how this worked.

"Yes," Darby said, her voice fierce. "That's exactly what I think you should do!"

Okay, she was upset, he'd known she would be. He gestured to the door. "Let's go downstairs, light a fire, order pizza, have a glass of wine."

"You want to eat?" Darby asked, incredulous.

Well, yeah. It had been a long, tough day. "Come downstairs, Darby."

Darby turned back to the window. "I need some time alone, Judah."

Judah walked over to her and wrapped his arm around her waist, pulling her into him. "I know this hurts, Darby. I know you love her. But this is the way it must be. We always knew this was going to happen."

"And us? Is this the end of us, too?"

"I don't want it to be," Judah admitted. "We're good together, Darby. We enjoy each other's company, we have great sex, this…works."

It worked? God, what was the point of his very expensive education if he couldn't get the words out? It wasn't difficult: *I want you in my life. I need you. I love you.*

They were just words, but the emotions behind

them felt as big as a Montana sky, as deep as a Norwegian fjord.

What if she said no? What if she wasn't feeling the same way? She loved Jac, he knew that, but did she love him? He didn't know, couldn't guess.

So he picked his way through this minefield of a conversation, wary to advance until he was sure of his position.

"We're going to miss Jac, but in a week or two, when we start adjusting to life without her—" the pain would recede, they'd be okay "—we can start anew. One of my oldest clients has bought a plot of land in Arizona, deep in the heart of the desert, and he wants me to design a house that complements its surroundings. I'd like you to come with me."

If nothing else, working, being creative, might distract them from the brown-eyed, rosy-cheeked smiler who would no longer be part of their lives.

"I have a business here, Judah. I can't just leave on a whim."

It would be a business trip, for both of them. He valued her opinion as a professional, he'd pay her as he would pay any other consultant. But now wasn't the time to go into that, he'd broach the subject again when they weren't feeling so raw.

"Let's go downstairs, Darby. Curl up by the fire, have some wine." And hopefully, that pizza. His stomach didn't care that his heart was bleeding and his brain felt like it was about to explode.

Darby shook her head, lifting her hand to place it

on the cold windowpane. Judah could feel her slipping further and further away from him, retreating behind that shield she erected to protect herself. He tightened his arms around her, trying to keep her anchored to him.

He wished she'd cry, scream, fight... She felt like a particularly brittle pane of glass in his arms.

"Darby, stay with me," he implored.

She didn't reply, and he buried his face in her neck, inhaling her scent. He hated to see her this hurt, couldn't bear to watch this brave, strong independent woman's heart breaking before his eyes. He'd do anything for her...

Even this.

"Darby, you can't have Jac, but if you want a baby, I'll give you one."

Shock rippled through her, a mini-earthquake. Her laugh, when it came, was forced and her words laced with disbelief. "Sorry. I thought you said that you'd give me a baby."

"I will." He turned her around, cupped her face in his hands and bent his knees so he could look directly into her eyes. "Instead of choosing a sperm donor, take me. Let's make a baby, together."

Darby bit the inside of her lip, her eyes troubled. "Why?"

Judah placed a kiss on her forehead, then dropped his lips to her mouth. So sweet, so sexy. His.

He pulled back, resting his forehead against hers.

"Because you want one, sweetheart. If you wanted the moon, I'd try to get it for you."

It was such a huge offer, unbelievably generous and gut-wrenchingly sincere.

On top of hearing that Jac was leaving, this was too much. Darby felt too exposed, like she was a piece of faulty wiring, sparking intermittently. She wanted to say yes, she wanted to scream no, she wanted to run, to hide, to roll her life back six weeks to when she was just faced with the reasonably easy choice of becoming a single mother or not.

Judah, Jac—they'd complicated her life beyond measure. Saying no was impossible, saying yes was too easy. He'd offered her everything she wanted but nothing she needed.

She was beyond confused and maybe it was better that words had deserted her. She had no idea what to say, how to act.

So Darby did the only thing that came naturally, took the only action she could. Lifting herself to her toes, she touched her mouth against his, gently skimming her lips across his, imprinting the feel of his mouth on her brain. Hooking her arm around his neck, she plastered her body to his, sighing when his hand skimmed up and under her sweatshirt and finding the bare skin of her hip, banding his arm under her butt cheeks to jerk her into his body. She was off her feet now, her breasts pushed into his chest as his tongue slid into her mouth, setting her world ablaze.

This. This was what she understood. Judah touching her, loving her. This made sense.

This she could do.

Darby wrapped her legs around his waist, trusting him to hold her while she pulled the sweatshirt up and over her head, so that she was fully naked in his arms. Dropping the garment to the floor, she looked into his eyes, watching as the color went from dark blue to a shade of black. It was the color of midnight seas and dark nights full of sin and sex.

Their gazes clashed and held and beneath the lust and the desire, she saw a deeper emotion, something that scared her, beckoning her to surrender, to fall under his spell. Tempted but terrified, Darby dropped her gaze to his sexy mouth and touched her lips to the shallow dimple at the side of his cheek, feeling his stubble on her tender skin. He smelled like snow and cologne, temptation and terror. She could give this man her heart, hand it over, it would be so easy to do…

Take it, take me. Love me as I love you.

The words hovered on her tongue but she swallowed them down, knowing that once they were out they couldn't be retrieved. No, she would speak with her mouth and hands, with her aching-for-his-touch body.

This she could have; this she could do.

Darby dropped her feet to the floor and stepped back, filling her fists with black cashmere and the fine white cotton of his collared shirt. She pulled the garments up his chest and Judah helped her by reaching back with one hand and tugging the shirt and sweater over his head in one fluid move.

Darby immediately put her hands on his chest, feelings his flat nipples under her palms. "You are so hot, Judah. I want you so much."

Judah sucked in a breath, standing stock-still as she trailed her fingers over his ribs, across his ridged stomach, ruffling the hair of his happy trail. Darby looked down and saw that his erection was tenting his pants, straining the fabric.

As if reading her mind, Judah lifted his hands to his belt buckle, but Darby shook her head, needing to do this, to love him right. Pushing his hands away, she put her fingers between the smooth skin of his abdomen and the band of his black pants, small, slight touches that brushed the tip of his cock, causing his breath to turn choppy.

She ignored, as best she could, his hand running down her hip and thigh, scooting closer and closer to her happy place. When his hand brushed her strip of hair, she pushed it away, not wanting to get distracted, to lose herself to pleasure.

Judah clenched his hands into fists but kept them at his sides, seeming to sense that this was the one area where she knew the right moves to make. She was angry and sad about Jac leaving, blown away by his offer to father her children, confused by what it all meant—but loving Judah, touching him, this she knew how to do.

Darby flicked open the snap on his pants, pushed her hands inside and pulled the fabric over his butt, down his hips. She looked down and there he was, straining upward, desperate for her touch.

Judah toed off his shoes and socks, kicked the garments away and just stood there, his eyes narrowed, his mouth taut.

Darby ran the tip of her finger down his shaft. "You are so damned beautiful, Judah. Everywhere."

"Darby."

Her name was a small word but he saturated it with need. Darby felt the moisture pool between her legs, stunned that she could be this turned on by just looking at Judah, from the briefest of touches.

She wrapped her hand around him, her other hand cupping his balls. She lifted her face. "Kiss me."

Her demand was rough and insistent, and Judah didn't hesitate. His mouth plundered hers, seeking and demanding everything she had. This was unlike any kiss they'd shared before, there was no finesse, no sophistication, just raw need. It was out of control, wild, perfectly passionate, hot, hungry.

Darby felt Judah lift her and when he lowered her to the bed she knew she was no longer in control... but, then again, neither was he.

He left her mouth to pull her nipple between his lips and she whimpered, arching her back so he could take more of her, to increase the pressure. He pulled away to lavish attention on her other breast but before he could, she wiggled down so that her tongue swiped across his nipple, a small smile blooming when that tiny bead contracted. Moving down his body, she rubbed her nose over the ridges of his stomach, allowing her lips to make brief contact with his tip...

Darby squawked when Judah released a muted roar and then she was on her back, his knee pushing her legs apart, the head of his erection probing her entrance.

His hands flat on the bed on either side of her head, he held himself still, his eyes blazing when he looked down into her. "Darby! Do you want this?"

"Yes." She gasped, lifting her hips, so close and needing completion.

Judah balanced on one hand and his other gently cradled her jaw. "Open your eyes."

Darby forced her eyelids up, trying to widen her legs, to make him come inside.

Didn't he understand she needed him? *Now.*

Judah shook his head. "Sweetheart, I need to know if this is okay, me without a condom?"

God, she hadn't even noticed, and she didn't care. Condom, no condom, she just wanted to shatter, to not think, just feel.

"Yes, dammit. I need you, Judah." Darby heard the sob that followed her words, but she didn't care. She'd sob, beg, plead, cry...anything to have him completing her. Judah, in her, loving her, taking her up and up, was the only thing in her life that made sense, the only thing she could trust.

He wanted her, she wanted him. Pure, simple truth.

Judah surged inside her and her sobs turned to pants. Darby locked her legs around his hips, skin on skin, heat on heat, unaware that tears rolled down her cheeks. She'd never imagined that he'd feel so perfect, so right.

Judah rocked into her and lifted her higher, rocked again and boosted her up a level. She couldn't take much more. It was too much, the pleasure so intense. Then Judah rotated his hips, hit a spot and she hurtled into that bright light that was both fire and ice, blissful and shockingly intense. From what felt like a galaxy away, she heard Judah's hoarse cry, felt him come and she shattered again.

Perfection. Pleasure. Judah.

Darby wrapped her arms around his head and held on, tears rolling down her cheeks and onto his face as they tumbled back to earth.

And reality.

Ten

Judah sent an email confirming that he and Jac would meet the private jet he'd hired to fly Jac back to Italy later that afternoon.

He leaned back in his chair and glanced over to the playpen where Jac sat, babbling nonsense to the soft yellow duck she adored. He'd be packing the yellow duck and her favorite blanket, but he'd leave everything else he'd purchased for Jac here in Boston.

Carla, ridiculously wealthy, had everything she needed, and maybe, sometime in the future, he and Darby could use all the baby equipment. It was, after all, brand-new.

Judah glanced across the room to where Darby sat on the couch, pretzel-style, her laptop in her lap. He'd woken up in an empty bed and went hunting for her and Jac. He found them in the spare room, curled up on the window seat, Jac lying on Darby's chest, fast asleep. Darby's eyes had been closed but he knew her too well to believe she was sleeping. But when she didn't open her eyes, he respected her silent appeal for some time alone with Jac, for some space.

Not wanting to push, they'd exchanged polite conversation throughout the morning. They'd addressed the subjects of work and the renovations on the buildings she wanted to sell, talking about the next steps needed regarding the art museum, that he was heading for New York after Italy to sign some contracts and to meet with a client.

On the surface, they were both acting like their world hadn't shifted, as if he hadn't offered to give her a child, both so very aware that she'd yet to give him an answer to his extraordinary proposal. He was savvy enough, mature enough to know that she'd ducked answering him by making love to him.

She'd handed over her body to him but not her biggest dream.

Knowing that Darby didn't like to be pushed, he'd given her most of the morning to broach the subject, but they were running out of time. Judah rubbed the back of his neck and steeled himself. This needed to be settled. It might as well be now.

"Darby, we need to talk."

Tension ran through her, as tangible as the snow still falling outside. "Can you manage on your own with her?" Darby asked, not looking up from her computer. "Should I come with you?"

He wanted to say yes, to give her more time with Jac, but he knew that would just delay the inevitable. Whether they said goodbye to Jac today or tomorrow morning in Como, it would still hurt the same.

"I'll be fine."

Darby jerked her head in acknowledgment but didn't meet his eyes.

Sighing, Judah pushed his chair back, walking around the desk to where she sat. When she didn't look up, he sat down on the sturdy coffee table and pulled her laptop out of her hands, firmly closing the lid. Darby scowled at him and folded her arms across her chest.

She brushed her hair off her forehead. "Don't forget to pack her duck and her pink blanket. What do you want me to do with the rest of her stuff? Have it shipped to Italy?" she asked, her voice brittle.

Judah leaned forward and allowed his hands to dangle between his thighs. "I'm hoping you'll keep it, that we'll eventually use it."

Darby stared at a point past his shoulder, pulling her bottom lip between her teeth, gray eyes darkening. She didn't speak, and Judah sighed.

"Are we seriously going to pretend that I didn't ask you to have my child?"

Darby's eyes flew back to his face and she shook her head. "You don't know what you are asking, Judah. It's not that simple."

"Okay, then explain it to me."

"IVF is an expensive process and the chances of it being successful the first time around are low. It's emotionally draining and mentally demanding. It's more than just offering me your sperm."

He wasn't an idiot, he understood that. Why did she make it sound like his boys were all that he was offering?

"Darby, I understand that. I didn't make the offer lightly. I want to do this for you."

Darby stared at him for a long time before shaking her head and pointing her finger at him. "There, that's the problem in a nutshell."

Judah rubbed his forehead, confused. "I really don't understand. Explain, for the love of God."

Darby pulled her feet up onto the couch and wrapped her arms around her shins. She rested her chin on one knee, her eyes locked on his. "In a perfect world, would you be making this offer?"

He couldn't lie to her. "No. I'd be asking you to travel with me, to explore the world, help me design spectacular buildings. Having kids is not my first choice."

Darby shot Jac a glance. "Even after the fun we've had, knowing how wonderful she is, how can you not want to have kids?"

Because having Jac was a fairy tale. They were playing house. It was a novelty, a step out of time. "It's not always this good, Darby. I know how tough raising a child can be."

Darby vehemently shook her head. "You know how tough it can be raising a kid when you are barely more than a kid yourself. You're still looking at that time with Jake through the lens of an exploited teenager. You're an adult, Judah, and we'd do it together."

Her words rocked him, and he felt off-kilter.

She was wrong, she had to be.

"Darby, I did this for six years and it's not like this, not all the time." He ran agitated fingers across his forehead, tapped his foot. And why was she fighting him, he was offering what she most wanted! "But you're missing the point, I said that I *would* do it, I would go through that again because you want a child. When I get back from New York, we'll see your specialist together, work out what we need to do next."

"You're missing *my* point, Judah," Darby said, her voice infinitely sad. "I'd rather do this alone than have you becoming a father as a favor to me."

What?

No, wait, *what*?

Judah stared at her, unable to comprehend what she was telling him. Was that a no? Seriously? "I don't understand."

He loved her. Fully, completely, utterly. For as long as he lived, whatever he had was hers. He wanted to give her this thing she most wanted but she was saying no? If she didn't want to have a baby with him, how could he persuade her to accept his heart?

"You're just saying all this because you don't want to let me go."

Of course, he didn't want to let her slip away. What man in his right mind would?

Darby looked, if that was at all possible, paler than she did last night. "Do you know how tempting your offer is? You're smart and funny and gorgeous and I am so in love with you—"

He opened his mouth to tell her that he loved her, too, but she held up her hand, asking for his silence. "If I take you up on your offer, there's so much that could go wrong. I don't want to live with this niggling reminder that having a baby wasn't your first choice, that you are going through this horrible process for me. That you'll question whether the time and energy and money is worth it."

He tried to talk again but she spoke over him. "I heard about this couple, she wanted kids, he didn't. They had a baby and she felt resentful because he wasn't involved in raising their child. He said that he never wanted children, so why should he change a diaper or make a bottle?"

"That's not a fair comparison to make. I'm not like that."

"I don't know, Judah, we've only known each other a short time! Can you understand that your offer is too big, too encompassing, too quickly made?" Darby quietly asked. "This isn't a building, Judah, the shape of a roof, the placement of windows, something that can be redrawn, rebuilt if we make the wrong choice. We will be creating life. Do you understand that? It will be a life we will both be responsible for until the day we die, whether we want to be or not. My child, *our* child, deserves the very best we both have to offer, Judah, the best you have to offer. Saying you will *give* me a child is far from your best and I won't accept less than full involvement from you, or from any other man." Darby stood up. "I'd rather do this solo."

Judah stared at her, shocked. Feeling as if she'd ripped out his heart and ground it under the heel of one of her designer shoes. He felt both sick and supremely…pissed.

Hurt. Frustrated. Soul deep angry.

Did she not understand how hard it was for him to make that offer, how much he loved her to even consider *having* a child? He was prepared to give up his freedom, a considerable amount of cash, his time to do this with her…but she was refusing.

Stubborn, contrary woman.

Because anger was easier to deal with than pain, he lashed out. "Are you sure your motives about having a child are that pure, Darby?"

Darby frowned at him, caught off guard. "What are you talking about?"

"You have all the answers—" damn good answers but he would die before he admitted that to her "—but maybe a part of you only wants a child because it's the only thing you've ever failed at."

Darby looked like he'd plunged a knife into her chest. He should get up and walk away, but the words flew off his tongue. "Maybe this need to have a child is all about having control, about proving it to yourself that you can and less about your mothering instinct. You're prepared to toss us away, an exciting dynamic life, to change diapers and make bottles and be restricted and confined. Do you know how stupid that is?"

When fire flashed in her eyes, he knew that *stupid* had been the wrong word to use. Hell, all his words were asinine; he knew it even as he said them.

"You're on thin ice, Huntley."

Yet he still couldn't stop, the anger, the loss, was too much. "I offered you the one thing I never wanted in order to make you happy, but you tossed it in my face."

"Then you went on to question my motive for wanting a child. Don't forget that!" Darby leaped to her feet, her expression wild.

"If you were so sure you wanted kids, you would've made the decision to have IVF months ago and not thought twice about it!"

Judging by her shaking hands and wobbly bottom lip, Judah knew that he'd pushed a very big button.

"That's not fair, Judah," Darby whispered, in a voice so broken it caused his throat to close.

"So much about life isn't, Darby," Judah muttered.

A small wail pulled their attention away from their argument and back to Jac. They both stepped toward the playpen, but Darby reached the red-faced and sobbing child first. She picked her up, cuddled the baby to her chest and swayed from side to side.

At that moment, seeing her instinctive urge to comfort, Judah realized that in his anger, he'd made a very big error. She was smart, talented, so very driven, but yes, she was born to have it all. The career, the success, the child…the children.

"Shhh, baby," Darby murmured and Jac's sobs lessened. Then Jac tucked her face into Darby's neck, wrapped her little hand around a lock of her hair and pulled it to her cheek. Her eyes closed, and she was instantly fast asleep.

Darby kissed her little face, hugged her once more and placed her back on the mattress in the playpen. Pulling Jac's pink blanket over her tiny body, she touched her fingers to her lips before placing them back on Jac's little head. "I love you, baby girl. I hope you find your happy."

Darby's eyes skittered over Judah before she looked away. "She's all yours."

Judah watched, his heart breaking, as Darby walked out the door and, he presumed, out of his life.

Radio silence from Mason. Again.

Callie, pulling her earbuds out of her ears, stopped outside the front door to Mason's coffee shop and squinted at the glass doorway. Four days had passed since Mason walked out of her life, since she'd seen him, spoken to him.

She'd said what she needed to, told him where she stood. But the man had yet to tell her what he needed, what he was thinking or what he wanted.

Callie rested her back against the wall and lifted her foot, placing her sneaker on the wall behind her. The neighborhood was quiet this time of the morning. Few people chose to rise this early, but since she was awake anyway, she thought she might as well get some exercise.

Callie looked around with fresh eyes. While she and Ray had traveled extensively, she hadn't lived anywhere else but here. She'd miss this place, of course she would. She'd miss her children more. But she needed to leave, to be someone other than her kids' mom, Ray's widow.

Mason would have to stay here, for a year or two at least, until his youngest son completed school.

Callie looked up at the bright bold blue of the winter sky and sighed. She wanted to keep Mason in her life, but she didn't want a long-distance relationship. That wasn't fair to either of them. She could ask him to join her when he could but who knew where she'd be, what she'd be doing, whom she might meet between then and now?

There was only today. She couldn't make plans that far into the future. She needed to go, he needed to stay, so…maybe it was time to let Mason go.

Callie heard the rumble of Mason's Jeep and turned her head to the right, watching as he steered the black SUV into his customary parking spot. Switching off the engine, he stepped out and slammed the door closed. He leaned back against his vehicle and looked at her, those deep eyes serious.

"I'm in love with you."

Callie pushed her sunglasses up into her hair, wishing he hadn't said the words. Knowing he felt the same way she did would make leaving so much harder.

"I didn't want to fall in love with you, it wasn't the plan." Mason rolled his big shoulders. "You were supposed to be another diversion." His eyes moved from her to the windows of his shop, his expression a mixture of exasperation and amusement. "This worked for me, for a few years. After the stress of my previous job, making cappuccinos and lattes felt like heaven. I had time for my kids, time to work out, to chill. It felt right. It *was* right."

Callie placed her palms against the wall and her breathing turned shallow. Where was he going with this?

"Fair warning, if we do this, you'll be the one making coffee. All the time. I'm done with coffee shops."

Callie bit the inside of her lip as her throat closed. With fear or anticipation. A little bit of both. "What are we going to do, Mason?"

Mason folded his arms across his chest and Callie noticed the lines around his mouth were deeper, his eyes worried. For the first time ever, Mason seemed to be feeling a little out of his depth. Seeing that, strangely, relaxed her. She wasn't the only one, as Levi would say, with skin in the game, and that was reassuring.

"My kids were my greatest worry, my biggest challenge. I've had custody of them since I got divorced, although my ex is very involved in their lives. I've spent a lot of time thinking about how I can have them and you. How can I make this work?"

"Your kids come first, Mace. That's not up for discussion," Callie said, her tone fierce. She would not be the person who came between Mason and his sons.

"Emmet will be off to college in a few months and Teag has another eighteen months before he goes, too. The boys like their stepdad, they all get along well. I might have custody, but my boys spend as much time with Karen and Doug as they do with me." He pulled in a breath. "So, my ex and her husband are happy for the boys to come and live with them, in fact they are all damn excited." A small smile touched Mason's lips. "When I am in the country, the boys will stay with me, obviously."

In the country? What? "I don't understand."

Mason folded his arms against his chest. "I want to come traveling with you, Cal. Provided we don't go mad, I earn enough from my investments to cover my obligations to the boys and to live comfortably. If I need more money, or get bored, there are university departments all over the world who'd be interested in having me as a guest lecturer, organizations that would hire me to solve some of their trickier problems."

"You and your big brain," Callie murmured, feeling the need to tease him. It was either that or cry. She felt overwhelmed, terrified, so happy she wanted to burst out of her skin.

"The point is, I could travel with you, I *want* to travel with you." Mason rubbed the back of his neck. "If that's something you might be interested in."

Something she *might* be interested in? Really?

It was only a dream come true.

"I know you want to find yourself, carve out your own identity, be Callie. I don't want to stop you from doing that, from doing whatever you want to do." Mason's voice held a hint of panic. "I just want to watch you while you do it. But I understand if it's something you need to do alone. I won't like it, but I'll understand."

This man…this amazing, supersmart, hot man. He just got her.

Mason didn't want to change her. He wanted to love her while she explored the next phase of her life. It was an enormous gift, a marvelous realization. She could do anything, be anything and Mason would be there, standing behind her.

Callie wanted to go to him but there were still words to be said, conditions to be discussed. "I would love for you to come traveling with me, Mace, to be with me, more than anything in the world. But I think you should know, now, that I'm never going to marry you. I'm going to love you, probably until I die, but I'm not going to marry you."

"I'm good with that." Mason nodded, his eyes

filled with amusement. "That way I'll always know you're with me because you want to be and not because a piece of paper says you have to be. I'm especially happy about the you-loving-me part." He pretended to wipe a bead of sweat off his forehead. "That's a bit of a relief."

"I think I fell in love with you when you first offered to help me out with my bucket list," Callie admitted.

Mason's eyes were steady on her face, his expression all sincere tenderness. "You are the adventure I've been waiting for, Cal."

There was nothing she wanted more than to step into his arms, to embrace her future, but she still had words to say. She held up her hand. "Wait. I'm not done."

"Make it sharp, Brogan, I need to kiss you." Mason rolled his index finger in a gesture that told her to hurry up.

"No matter where we are, what we are doing, we come back to Boston every year for three months in the summer. And for two weeks over Christmas. That's family time, yours and mine. We spend that time with our kids, either together or apart. But we see our kids, twice a year. That's not negotiable."

Mason's expression turned back to tender. "I'm so behind that. Anything else?"

"No." Callie allowed her smile to bloom, feeling like the luckiest woman in the world. She'd had a husband who loved her, and now she had a lover and a partner to spend the rest of her life with. How lucky was she to be loved by two amazing men?

As Mason put his hands on her hips to pull her to him—God, he felt so good—she slapped her hands on his chest, laughter bubbling. "Apparently, Mrs. Jenkins saw my impromptu striptease the other day. Half the neighborhood is wondering what kind of hanky-panky was happening in your coffee shop. The other half is convinced she's nuts."

"Nobody suspects you?" Mason murmured.

"I don't do public displays of affection, everyone knows that." Callie made her voice deliberately prim. "It's not what good girls do."

"Such a liar." Mason, deliberately, cupped her breast and swiped her nipple, his mouth an inch from hers. "The real Callie Brogan isn't a good girl, she's a hot wild strong woman. And I'm nuts about her."

Mason's thumb moved up her neck, across her jaw. "There's a group of joggers at the top of the street. Behind them is Mrs. Jenkins on her scooter. Want to give them something new to talk about?"

Laughter skittered through Callie. She lifted her face up, brushed her lips against Mason's mouth. "Oh, yes, please. PDA the hell out of me, Mace."

Eleven

Darby forced herself to work, to tie up all the loose ends outstanding for Huntley and Associates, pushing from minute to minute, hour to hour.

Even so, her thoughts kept drifting to Jac, wondering if the little girl knew that her little life was about to take another detour, wondering if she was old enough to miss Darby or Judah. But then thoughts of Jac took Darby to thoughts of Judah—as if she could *not* think about him!—and she wondered how he was holding up.

Despite their fight, his ridiculous belief that he didn't want children, she knew that handing over Jac would rip his heart in two. It was the right course of action—that fantastic ray of human sunshine had only been on loan to them—but no matter how stoic

Judah acted, Darby knew that taking Jac back to Carla would be difficult.

He'd insist on interviewing Jac's new nanny and Darby was pretty sure he'd offer the woman some additional cash to keep him informed about Jac's progress, to let him know if she needed anything, to send him photographs. To call him if Carla went off the rails again.

Jac might be his niece but she was also the child of his heart.

Curled up in the corner of the sofa in her mother's house, Darby looked up when Jules walked into the room, dark hair glistening with moisture. Callie had called to check up on Darby and immediately knew that one of her chicks was in pain. She then called in reinforcements. There was a laptop on the coffee table and Darby knew DJ would be calling in soon from the Netherlands. When a crisis struck, the Brogan women didn't let a little thing like distance come between them and much-needed support.

Callie walked into the room carrying mugs of cocoa. Darby took her cup, looked down at the little marshmallows bobbing in the creamy richness and felt her throat gag. Her life, everything that mattered, was on a plane heading to Europe and her throat was tight, her stomach cramping. Darby placed her mug on the table and rested her head on the back of the sofa, closing her eyes.

She heard the incoming Skype call, DJ's voice, but didn't open her eyes. She didn't want to face this moment, this life that didn't have Judah or Jac in it. Her two Js, the loves of her life.

Callie sat down next to Darby, placed her hand on her thigh and Darby opened her eyes to look into Callie's bright blue eyes.

"I'm okay, Mom," she said, because she felt she had to. She was a strong independent woman…

Who felt like her heart had been ripped in two.

"Has Jac gone back?" DJ asked.

Darby looked at the laptop screen and nodded. "Carla is at home and she's hired a nanny."

"You knew this day would come," Jules softly said.

Darby couldn't argue with that. "I did, and I thought I could handle it." She shrugged. "Turns out I can't."

They all turned at the sound of footsteps in the hallway and Darby was surprised to see Levi walking into the living room and not Mason. Running a hand through his damp hair, he looked at Darby with worry on his face. "Mom called, said that Jac and Judah had left." He shuffled from foot to foot. "I wanted to see if you were okay."

Darby was touched by his concern. She'd managed to contain her tears with Callie and Jules but knowing that her big brother had left work early to check up on her flipped the switch to make the waterworks flow.

"Oh, crap." Levi held up his hands. "Sorry. I'll go."

Darby shook her head and held out her hand to

JOSS WOOD   193

him, frantically wiping her face with her other hand. Levi walked across the room and sat down on the arm of the sofa and Darby leaned into him, needing his strength.

She felt his hand on her head and forced the words over her tongue. "He offered to give me a baby."

DJ was the first to respond with a loud "woo-hoo!"

Callie grinned and Jules wiped an imaginary bead of sweat off her brow. "Yay, no sperm donors. He's hot and smart and yeah, we like him."

Darby looked up to see Levi's reaction. Of the three of them who knew her so well, it was her brother who immediately understood that Judah's offer wasn't welcome.

"You want a baby, Judah has said that he'll give you one. What's the problem?" Levi asked, frowning.

Darby lifted one shoulder and played with the ring on her middle finger. "Judah doesn't want a child and is only offering because he wants me to be happy."

Jules's face softened. "Oh, that's so romantic. He loves you."

Maybe he did. She understood their confusion: a gorgeous man was offering her a relationship and a child. Her perfect, much-dreamed-about life was a yes away and she was crying. It shouldn't make sense, but it did, to her.

Darby shook her head. "He cares for me, I admit that. But you know me, I'm not prepared to settle."

Jules and Callie exchanged a confused look. "How

would you be settling?" Callie asked before lifting her mug to her mouth.

"His idea of a perfect relationship is different than mine. He wants us to travel, to design buildings, to be childless and free. My idea of a perfect relationship is a house we've both designed together, having a career while raising a passel of kids. A husband that is fully committed to our life, to me, to his kids."

"You're worried that if you have children together, he might feel resentful, that he will put his career, and not you and your children, first," Levi stated.

Darby nodded. "I could, almost, maybe, play second fiddle to his career—"

"Oh, you could not!" Jules interrupted.

"Maybe not," Darby admitted. "But I know myself, if we had children and he wasn't the type of dad to them I know he can be, if he didn't give them his all, I'd lose respect for him. And that wouldn't be fair because I knew how he felt going in."

She continued, "I also think that if we go through this process, this difficult and expensive process, to have children and we didn't give them everything we had as parents, that would be—" Darby searched for the word "—I don't know the exact word I'm looking for...*immoral? Unfair?* No, I think I'd prefer to do it on my own."

When none of her family responded, Darby wondered if she was overthinking this, whether she'd been too analytical, too hard. She hoped they wouldn't try to change her mind because she would be easily tempted to take a chance, to try it Judah's way.

She loved him that much. She didn't want to be without him.

But a voice deep in her soul, that part of her connected with the earth and the universe and whatever life force that created her, insisted she shouldn't. It was better to find another way to have the babies she so desperately wanted.

If she actually wanted babies and not control.

She couldn't get Judah's words out of her head, had turned them over and over again. Examined them from every angle. Darby ran her hands down her thighs, wrinkled her nose and looked up at Levi. He'd tell her straight; he wouldn't try to cushion his words. Levi was unflinchingly honest.

"Judah said I want children because I like control, because I haven't failed at anything else and that I don't want to fail at this either."

Levi lifted his eyebrows and fury darkened his eyes.

She held up her hand, not needing his protection but his honesty. "Do you think he's right?"

Callie opened her mouth to speak but Darby kept her hand up and her eyes on Levi. She wanted his opinion.

Levi opened his mouth, closed it and rubbed the back of his neck. "I think it's a factor."

Darby ignored the protests from her female backup team and slowly nodded. She placed the balls of her hands into her eye sockets and tried to push the pain away. She dropped her hands, opened her eyes and watched as Callie and her sisters argued with Levi, who didn't try to defend himself. He just sat there, absorbing their ire, his eyes on her face.

When she couldn't take any more, Darby lifted her hand. "He's right."

It took a long moment for her words to sink in. When silence dropped into the room like a heavy wet blanket, she looked at her mom, then Jules, then DJ, making eye contact with each of them before leaning into Levi's thigh.

"He's right, so is Judah. Not a hundred percent, but a little bit right."

Callie frowned. "I don't understand, Darby."

"I didn't either, until Judah had the balls to say it. It's something I've been battling with over the past few months, but I wouldn't put my fears into words, so I couldn't identify it." Darby stood up and walked to the fireplace, picking up a photograph of her, Levi and Jules, taken when they were toddlers. Jules sat in Levi's lap, her arms around her middle and Darby stood next to them, a small gap between her and Levi.

"I've always been competitive, it's a part of my nature. You are our father's son, Levi, but I am his daughter." She turned and looked at her brother, holding the frame of the photo. "You and Jules always had this special bond. My earliest memories of you are of me, wanting that bond with you."

Levi nodded, a small gesture, but Darby took it as encouragement. It was time to lance the wound, to allow all the poison to escape.

"When I was seven, you gave Jules a music box for Christmas. You gave me, God, a ratty baseball card."

"You threw a hissy fit and wouldn't come out of your room for the rest of the day. I couldn't understand what I did wrong. You'd just started to play baseball and that was my favorite card."

It had been mangled and torn and, yeah, ugly. What had she been supposed to think? But he'd thought he was doing something nice, she'd been insulted. Darby shook her head. Boys. She'd never understand them.

"I saw the disparity in the gifts as you loving Jules more, something I'd long suspected. That Christmas Day I vowed that I would never be second-best, that I would always, always be first and maybe, someday, you would love me as much as you loved her."

"God, Darby," Levi muttered, standing up. He walked over to her and pulled her into his chest, holding her against his big body.

Darby sucked in his strength, wanting to stand there forever, but she pushed him away, determined to get this done. She knew her mom and sisters were crying and she couldn't look at them because then she'd totally lose it. "So, my competitive streak was born. Recently, when I heard that my time was running out to have IVF, I suddenly got cold feet. This was my goal, why couldn't I pull the trigger? What if I failed? What if it didn't work? What if I only wanted to become a mom because I didn't want to fail?"

Levi dropped to the rug and pulled Darby down so she was sitting opposite him, mirroring his crossed legs. He placed his big hands on her knees and looked into her eyes, the green of his brilliant in the soft light.

When he spoke, his voice was a low soothing rumble. "Even as a little girl, you were so damn fierce, so very independent." His mouth quirked at the corners. "So damn opinionated. Jules allowed me to protect her, to play the older brother, you refused to. I couldn't help you over puddles, you'd plow through them. I'd tell Jules that a tree was too dangerous to climb. She'd listen. You? You climbed higher. You were fearless, determined, God, so annoying. I couldn't protect you because you wouldn't let me protect you and it drove me nuts, it *still* drives me nuts."

He took a breath and continued, "For any pain I caused you, I'm sorry. I should've found another way to deal with you, to make you feel as special as Jules, but that doesn't mean I love you less than Jules. Frankly, all three of you are pains in my ass."

Muted laughter dissolved some of the tension.

"But to come back to your question about whether you are having kids because you're competitive…"

Darby held her breath, worried that he would confirm her worst fears about herself.

"Is your competitive streak a factor in wanting to have kids? Sure it is. But it's not your driving force. Beneath your bossy ways, you're a nurturer, but because you are strong and independent, people don't see it."

Levi carried on. "You'd be a fearless mom, Darby, because you are fearless. You'd be the mom climbing trees, playing in the sand, learning to surf. Because you are independent and strong, you'll raise strong and independent girls and you'll raise your sons to respect strong and independent women. You want kids because you have something to give them, Darby, don't doubt that. And yeah, I agree with you. You can't settle with Judah. You'd resent him for it and he'd resent himself for doing it. You're the type of people who don't ever settle, and love, well, love shouldn't ever involve settling for less than the very best."

Darby nodded, knowing he was right. She bit her bottom lip, knowing her tears were about to fall. "It hurts, Levi."

Levi hauled her into his arms, rocking her gently. "I know, honey, I really do. Love—having it and losing it—hurts like hell."

In Carla's luxurious lakeside villa, Judah held Jac in his arms, unable to hand her over, to let her go.

Carla, as he'd expected, showed little interest

in Jac and had languidly introduced him to Jac's new nanny. While Carla lay on a sofa bed, flicking through a magazine, looking pale and disinterested, Judah, keeping a firm hold on Jac, interrogated Joa, Jac's new nanny.

The woman, in her mid to late twenties, was tougher than she looked and held up well to his barrage of questions. Her credentials were solid and she'd passed the background check with flying colors. She seemed warm, capable and organized, and Jac liked her. Hell, if he had permanent custody of Jac, Joa was exactly the type of nanny he would've hired to look after his little girl.

He liked Joa, he did. It was Carla he had the problem with.

Judah looked at his ex and while he felt sorry for her, he had to wonder what he'd ever seen in her. She was stunning, sure, but self-absorbed and selfish. He'd stuck around, he suddenly realized, because he knew Carla was no threat to his single status, because he knew that, with her, he'd never be faced with the question of whether he should settle down, whether he loved her enough to commit to her, to plan a life with her.

That gray-eyed feisty blonde back home was the only one who'd ever managed to make him change his way of thinking.

Home, he'd used that word to refer to Boston. Was that where his home was now? Judah thought about that for a minute. Home was wherever Darby was. He loved her.

How the hell was he going to live his life without her?

He didn't think he could let Jac go either, not now or ever. She was his, as was Darby.

They were his girls and he needed to fight for them, fight for this life he'd never expected to want. The house filled with naughty boys and girls; their smart, hot mom who would not only help Judah create buildings but more important, create his life. A life filled with kids, and pets, and love and arguments and fantastic sex—

"I think it's time, Mr. Huntley," Joa said.

It was. It had been time for the last half hour.

Judah tightened his grip on Jac and lifted his free hand to grip the bridge of his nose. Handing Jac over was the legal thing to do but it wasn't the right thing to do.

Jac was his. And Darby's...

God, how could he make this work? What could he say that would allow him to leave with Jac? What argument would work with Carla?

Judah heard the door to the sunroom open and he saw Luca, Carla's manager, walk into the room, followed by a young man who looked like... Jesus, was that Jake?

Judah, keeping a firm hold on Jac, leaped to his feet, his eyes sweeping over his younger brother. Jake looked nothing like the thin, haggard, addicted man he'd last seen eighteen months ago. His dark hair was longer than Judah's and his eyes were a lighter shade of blue but, thank God, clear of drugs. His face had filled out, as had his body. He looked strong and healthy.

Relief swept through Judah, then anger. "Where the hell have you been? I heard you left rehab, that you disappeared."

He expected Jake to lash back but he just walked toward Judah, his hand held out to shake. "It wasn't working for me, so I decided to try something else."

Jake looked disappointed that Judah didn't shake his hand but he didn't say anything, just dropped his hand, then bent at the knees to look at Jac. "So, this is Jacquetta. She's beautiful."

He and Carla were pretty people, what the hell did he expect?

"What are you doing here, Jake?" Judah demanded. He glanced at Carla, who didn't look remotely surprised to see Jake. "Will someone tell me what the hell is going on?"

Luca lifted his eyebrows. "So, those rumors that your brother was in the area weren't wrong. Apparently—" Luca frowned at Carla "—Carla thought it would be a good idea to let the world think she was having an affair with Bertolli while sneaking off to see Jake."

Judah rolled his eyes at Luca and was rewarded with a small smile. His ex and his brother fed off drama.

"Then my appendix burst, and Jake spent the last two weeks sneaking into my hospital room late at night to see me," Carla said, sending Jake a grateful look that appeared, holy crap, full of love.

Oh, God, were these two back together?

Judah looked inside himself and realized he didn't care. He only cared about Jac. He glanced down and saw that Jac had fallen asleep in his arms. He couldn't give her up; he wouldn't.

Jake was an addict and while he might be clean now, the chances of him slipping back into addiction were high. As much as Judah liked Joa, he couldn't put Jac back into a house inhabited by two highly unstable and volatile people.

He was about to tell them that he was taking Jac, that they could fight him for custody, when Jake surprised Judah by walking over to Carla and dropping to his knees in front of her. She looked at him, defiance in her eyes.

"Carla. You need to make this decision, babe."

Judah looked at Joa, who lifted her eyebrows, seeming to be as confused as he was. He turned to Luca, who just shook his head, silently asking him to wait. Okay, he would wait, but not for long. In five minutes, he would be walking out with Jac—maybe with Joa, too—and to hell with the consequences. Though a spell in an Italian jail for kidnapping didn't appeal, it was a risk he was willing to take.

"Honey, we've spoken about this," Jake quietly stated. "When you told me that you spoke to Judah,

I thought you discussed the possibility of leaving her with him, not him bringing her back."

What. The. Hell? Judah didn't understand any of this. It sounded like they were talking about letting him leave with Jac. Letting him *have* Jac…

Carla bit her lip. "But people will think I am terrible, that I gave up my daughter."

"They'll think you handed your daughter over to her father and I'm sure Judah will allow you visitation rights."

"But you're her father!" Carla wailed. "You and I made her!"

Jake stood up and looked down at her, love and regret on his face. "Honey, you and I, we're not good for her. We're not what she needs. We're too broken, too damaged… That's why we understand each other so well. If Jacquetta stays with us, we'll just raise another broken soul and I've caused enough damage to enough people. I don't want to do that anymore."

Jake turned to Judah and in his brother's eyes, he saw the child who'd adored him, the boy he remembered. "You were a better father, a better man as a twelve-year-old than both Dad and me put together. You were incredible and still are today… I both love and hate you. I love you for looking after me, I hate you for leaving, although I understand why you did it."

Judah swallowed down the emotion. "You do?"

Jake's eyes radiated understanding. "You needed a life, Judah. The one you were living, looking after me, was killing you. I made my own choices, I knew better, even at thirteen, to not do the things I did, but I did them anyway. Possibly to force you to come back."

"Jake." His brother's name on his lips was a plea for forgiveness.

"It's okay, Judah, it really is. You weren't my father, you were not responsible for me. When I'm sober and clearheaded, I understand that. I don't understand it when I'm using." Jake sighed. "I've been clean for a few months, but the temptation is always there, and I can't guarantee that I won't slide again. Carla is addicted to attention, to her career, to herself."

Carla shrugged. "He's right."

"Neither of us are remotely adult enough, responsible enough, to raise a child. We won't ever be," Jake quietly stated. He nodded at Luca, who walked over to the desk. "Luca has papers, signing over full custody of Jacquetta to you. Will you take her? Will you raise her, as you did me?"

Judah felt his heart slam into his chest. He wanted to say yes, to grab what they were offering and run.

"What if you change your mind? What if you want her back? What then?"

Luca spoke. "It's ironclad, I made sure of it. If you sign, they relinquish all rights to her. You can refuse visitation rights. You can bar them from having any contact with her until she's an adult. I don't expect you to take my word for it. We can send the documents to your attorney and have him examine the legalese if you are in doubt."

Judah looked down at Jac's downy head, her red cheeks and perfect mouth, and suddenly realized that without her, without more kids, he would become as self-absorbed as his brother, as Carla, as addicted to his work and lifestyle as they were to drugs and attention. He'd designed and built fantastic buildings all over the world, but they were bricks and mortar, cold steel. They had no soul.

He'd made the choice earlier to live his life differently, but this conversation with his brother cemented his resolution to do exactly that.

Of course, he'd take Jac. He'd love her and any other kids he and Darby were lucky enough to have. He would be a good dad. Even his messed-up, currently sober brother thought so.

It was now time to be a *great* dad—the dad, the man, Darby needed him to be.

Judah stepped over to the desk, pulled the document toward him, grateful it was written in English and contained the minimal amount of legal speak. It was as Luca said, a full-custody agreement, signing over Jac to him.

Not hesitating, Judah grabbed the nearest pen and dashed his signature across the page. He stared down at his scrawl, the thought hitting him that he now had a daughter.

He loved her. With all his heart.

He had his child, all he needed now to make his life complete was his woman.

* * *

Meet me at the northeast corner of the neighborhood in an hour. I'll bring coffee.

Why?

Don't be late, Judah's next text stated.

Darby accepted that she and Judah were unconventional, that their entire relationship was odd, but she didn't understand why Judah insisted on seeing her before breakfast on Monday morning. Why they had to meet at this deserted, undeveloped part of the neighborhood was beyond her. Darby pulled her car up next to Judah's SUV and shook her head.

Snow covered the ground and the windchill factor dropped the temperature to just above freezing, but Judah stood on top of the slope to her right, hatless, his hands shoved into the pockets of his heavy jacket.

Why was he here? Why was he standing there looking cold but determined? Why wasn't he in New York, as he said he'd be?

Despite hot air blowing from her heater, Darby shivered. There was little point in talking—to be together, one of them had to make a major life-changing sacrifice for the other—so wasn't it better just to go their separate ways?

Talking wouldn't find a solution… There was no solution.

Darby saw Judah pull his phone out of his pocket and seconds later, hers rang. Darby stared down at her phone, shaking her head. If she got out of the car, she'd run up that hill and throw herself into his arms and tell him she didn't want to lose him. She loved him. She'd do anything—have his babies, not have his babies—to have him in her life. They'd be happy, for a year, two, maybe four. Then the doubts would creep in, then resentment and regret. They'd end up hating each other.

No, it was better to walk away now, while there was still love and respect.

Darby took one last glance at Judah and told herself to put the car into Drive, to leave. Her phone dinged with an incoming text and she looked down at the lit screen.

Five minutes. Please?

Not giving herself any more time to think, Darby switched off the engine and opened the door. The cold slapped her in the face, but she forced herself to leave the car, instantly burying her face in her cashmere scarf.

This was ridiculous. If Judah wanted to talk, why couldn't they have a conversation back at the house or in her office over coffee? She was already miserable, she didn't need to be cold, as well.

Darby walked up the hill, glad she was wearing flat boots with a decent grip. If she fell on her butt, she would be even more unhappy than she already was. And she was plenty unhappy…

When she reached Judah, he held out his bare hand, which Darby ignored. She stared out over the incredible view of rolling land. It had been years since she'd been up to this remote area. The architect in her noted that the plot of land had a helluva view. She knew Noah had plans to develop this area at some point. She remembered him saying something about retaining this land for very exclusive high-end buyers. Hopefully, she might, with her connection to the developer, be asked to design one or two of the houses.

But that was for the future, the future without Judah.

"Care to tell me why I am freezing my butt off?" Darby demanded, her tone as cold as the air swirling around them.

God, he looked so big and warm and wonderful. How was she going to stand watching him walk out of her life again?

"Noah is prepared to sell this land."

So?

"To me. I made him an offer and he accepted," Judah quietly stated, his voice low and slow. "I know exactly what I'd build here."

He had a client, someone Noah had recommended no doubt. Maybe Judah wanted to consult with her again. She could be his point person while he took on bigger and better projects all over the world.

No.

He'd have to find another local architect. In order to survive him leaving her life, he needed to leave her life. Utterly. Completely.

Darby had zero interest in the property or any of Judah's plans. Thinking of a future free of Judah felt like a red-hot dagger rhythmically plunging into her gut. "I can't work with you, Judah. Yes, being associated with you is wonderful for my career, but it hurts too much knowing there's no way for us to be together." Darby gestured to her car. "Can I go now? I'm freezing."

Judah's hand on her shoulder stopped her from walking away. "I'd build something long, something with glass and wood and steel."

Judah turned her so she faced the snow-covered fields and the woods at the end of the property. Darby knew that, on a clear day, they could see the sea.

"We'd wake up to this view every morning, but I'd give it not much more than a passing glance because all my attention would be on a gray-eyed blonde with messy hair, thanking God that she's in my life."

Darby stepped away from him, tipping her head back to look into his blazing eyes, blue fire in his pale face.

"What did you say?" she quietly asked, her heart slamming against her rib cage.

"I'd try to cop a feel, get you half-naked, but I'm pretty sure one of our kids would demand our attention before I got to the fun stuff. We'd argue about whose turn it is to get up and deal with our brood, but I'd go just because you smiled at me. Just because I'd be so damn happy to have you, to have our kids, to have our life."

Darby heard the sincerity in his voice, could see her dreams in his eyes, but she held up her hands, yanking herself out of the spell he'd put her under. "Judah, don't. Please don't."

"Please don't what?" Judah asked, still not touching her, his eyes still connected with hers.

"Don't show me the dream I so desperately want but can't have," Darby whispered.

Darby felt Judah's hand on her cheek, his thumb stroking her jaw. "I'm offering it to you, Darby, all you have to do is take it. We can build our dream house here, fill it with kids. Don't walk out of my life, Darby. Stay and live your dream."

He still didn't get it. "I don't want it to be my dream, Judah, I want it to be ours. I want you to want that, too, but you don't!"

Judah looked at her for a long moment before a tiny smile lifted the corner of his lips. He pointed to a huge oak, its thick branches now devoid of leaves. "I want to hang a tire swing from those branches for Jac, take her tadpole hunting in the creek behind the house. I see her catching lightning bugs in that field."

He spoke as if Jac would be a permanent part of his life. "What are you trying to tell me, Judah?"

Judah rubbed the back of his neck, looking frustrated. "Okay, I'm obviously not explaining properly. I want to build a house here, on this land, with you. For us and Jac. And any other children we might have. I'll still have to travel but you and our kids can come with me. If you stay behind, I'll make damn sure I'm back within a week, ten days. I want you to carry on working, with me or by yourself, I don't care."

Darby looked at him, poleaxed.

"I want your dream, Darby. The house, the kids… you. It all starts and ends with you."

Darby ignored the white-hot bolt of joy hurtling through her and focused on Judah's eyes. There was no hesitation there, no fear. He was telling the truth. He wanted the life he'd described. He genuinely wanted what she did.

But before she could fall into the happiness he promised, Darby still felt the need to warn him about what he was getting into. "Judah, my fertility issues… It's not going to be easy."

Judah clasped the back of her neck and rested his forehead on hers. "Sweetheart, it might take some time, and cash, for us to have kids but I'm a hundred percent committed to the process. I will do whatever it takes for you to carry your own baby. This is a journey we are now on together. I promise you we'll find a way."

He'd mentioned Jac. Did that mean he wanted to fight for her? How? Was that even possible?

Before she could ask, Judah spoke again. "Until we manage to get you pregnant, I have another little girl who desperately needs a mom."

Darby stepped backward, slapping her hands to her cheeks. He'd hinted at having Jac, but she hadn't wanted to believe that was a possibility. Losing Jac had hurt almost as much as losing Judah.

"You have Jac? You can get her back? When? What's the plan?"

Judah smiled, his face full of love. "The plan is that I tell you that I love you, ask you to marry me and after you say yes, we'll head back to the house, where I strip you naked and have my way with you. Or you can have your way with me, I'm not picky."

Darby grinned.

"After a couple of hours of loving you, we'll head over to Callie's and drag our daughter out of her sticky fingers."

Wait…what? By the name of all things holy, what? He'd said so much, she couldn't take it all in. One thing at a time.

"Jac is at my mom's? You *have* her?"

Judah nodded. "It's a long, complicated story but the condensed version is that my brother and Carla, who are back together, signed over full custody to me. I'd like us to formally adopt Jac as ours. Do you want to do that with me?"

She needed about two seconds to think about that. "Um…*yes*." Darby couldn't help doing a happy dance in the snow. Her baby was back. Her little girl…

The urge to run down the hill to her car, to drive immediately to where she could hug her daughter was strong. But she and Judah still had some issues to deal with.

Darby tipped her head to one side. "You love me? You want to marry me and build a house for us?"

Judah shook his head. "Not only a house, a *life*. I want a life with you at the center of it, sweetheart."

"Judah, you're anti-marriage, anticommitment, antikids. You love your freedom," Darby stated, suddenly scared. What if he changed his mind? What if he gave her this dream life for a couple of years and then started feeling hemmed in, constrained?

"I love you more," Judah said, his voice cracking with emotion. "Darby, I'm not going to change my mind. I'm not going to leave you with a house and kids, go off on my own. I've had my freedom, seventeen years of it, and I'm done being alone. I want you and Jac and however many more kids come our way. I want you. I want us."

Darby, needing to touch him, threw her arms around him and stood on her toes to bury her face in his neck. Ignoring her tears, she held on tight, trying to make sense of the last ten minutes. As Judah's arms banded around her—as he pulled her into his warmth, into his heart, into the life he'd created for them—she abandoned understanding and allowed herself to feel.

She loved him.

Darby pulled herself off him, taking a step back. When Judah reached for her again, she held up her hands. "If you touch me, I won't be able to talk, and I need to, Judah… I need to speak."

Judah nodded, his beautiful eyes tender.

Darby pulled in a deep breath, blinked away her tears. "I love—" Her voice cracked, and she cleared her throat. She lifted one shoulder and tried to smile. "I love you. I could've lived without you, just as you could've lived without me—we are strong enough people to do that but, God, it would've hurt. I would've been miserable because having you in my life... You *make* my life." Trying to smile, she looked at him, her breath catching in her throat. "I want you, too. And yes, please, I'd love to be your wife. I want the life I see in your eyes."

Judah's smile was slow to come but when it did, it warmed her, on that freezing morning, from the inside out. He reached for her, lifting her off her toes, his laughter a low rumble. One arm held her under her butt, his other hand held the back of her head, their mouths aligned. "Fair warning, I'm going to kiss the hell out of you now."

Darby grinned. "Strangely, I'm okay with that."

"Then we'll get out of this freezing wind and we'll pick up our daughter and take her home."

Darby kissed Judah before pulling her mouth away. "We don't want to upset my mom by picking her up too soon. Maybe we can wait a couple of hours before we head over."

Judah's eyes deepened with laughter and passion. "I can't think what we might do to fill the time," he teased.

Darby pretended to think. "I'm sure it will come to us. We are, after all, reasonably intelligent."

Judah brushed her hair off her face. "You and I, Darby? Smartest decision ever made."

Darby absolutely agreed.

* * * * *

Get 4 FREE REWARDS!

We'll send you 2 FREE Books plus 2 FREE Mystery Gifts.

Harlequin® Desire books feature heroes who have it all: wealth, status, incredible good looks... everything but the right woman.

FREE
Value Over
$20

YES! Please send me 2 FREE Harlequin® Desire novels and my 2 FREE gifts (gifts are worth about $10 retail). After receiving them, if I don't wish to receive any more books, I can return the shipping statement marked "cancel." If I don't cancel, I will receive 6 brand-new novels every month and be billed just $4.55 per book in the U.S. or $5.24 per book in Canada. That's a savings of at least 13% off the cover price! It's quite a bargain! Shipping and handling is just 50¢ per book in the U.S. and 75¢ per book in Canada.* I understand that accepting the 2 free books and gifts places me under no obligation to buy anything. I can always return a shipment and cancel at any time. The free books and gifts are mine to keep no matter what I decide.

225/326 HDN GMYU

Name (please print)

Address   Apt. #

City   State/Province   Zip/Postal Code

Mail to the Reader Service:
IN U.S.A.: P.O. Box 1341, Buffalo, NY 14240-8531
IN CANADA: P.O. Box 603, Fort Erie, Ontario L2A 5X3

Want to try 2 free books from another series! Call 1-800-873-8635 or visit www.ReaderService.com.

HD19R

He would never forget the day, ten years ago, when Maya
Richardson had walked through his door looking for a
job. She'd been a godsend, helping Ayden grow Stewart
Investments into the company it was today. Thinking
of her brought a smile to Ayden's face. How could it
not? Not only was she the best assistant he'd ever had,
Maya had fascinated him. Utterly and completely. Maya
had hidden an exceptional figure beneath professional
clothing and kept her hair in a tight bun. But Ayden had
often wondered what it would be like to throw her over
his desk and muss her up. Five years ago, he hadn't gone
quite that far, but he had crossed a boundary.

Maya had been devastated over her breakup with her
boyfriend. She'd come to him for comfort, and, instead,
Ayden had made love to her. Years of wondering what
it would be like to be with Maya had erupted into a

passionate encounter. Their one night together had been so explosive that the next morning Ayden had needed to take a step back to regain his perspective. He'd had to put up his guard; otherwise, he would have hurt her badly. He thought he'd been doing the right thing, but Maya hadn't thought so. In retrospect, Ayden wished he'd never given in to temptation. But he had, and he'd lost a damn good assistant. Maya had quit, and Ayden hadn't seen or heard from her since.

Shaking his head, Ayden strode to his desk and picked up the phone, dialing the recruiter who'd helped him find Carolyn. He wasn't looking forward to this process. It had taken a long time to find and train Carolyn. Before her, Ayden had dealt with several candidates walking into his office thinking they could ensnare him.

No, he had someone else in mind. A hardworking, dedicated professional who could read his mind without him saying a word and who knew how to handle a situation in his absence. Someone who knew about the big client he'd always wanted to capture but never could attain. She also had a penchant for numbers and research like no one he'd ever seen, not even Carolyn.

Ayden knew exactly who he wanted. He just needed to find out where she'd escaped to.

Don't miss what happens next!
At the CEO's Pleasure *by Yahrah St. John,*
part of her Stewart Heirs series!

Available January 2019 wherever
Harlequin® Desire books and ebooks are sold.

www.Harlequin.com

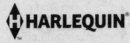

Love Harlequin romance?

DISCOVER.

Be the first to find out about promotions, news and exclusive content!

f Facebook.com/HarlequinBooks

🐦 Twitter.com/HarlequinBooks

📷 Instagram.com/HarlequinBooks

📌 Pinterest.com/HarlequinBooks

ReaderService.com

EXPLORE.

Sign up for the Harlequin e-newsletter and download a free book from any series at **TryHarlequin.com.**

CONNECT.

Join our Harlequin community to share your thoughts and connect with other romance readers!
Facebook.com/groups/HarlequinConnection

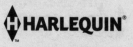

HARLEQUIN®

**ROMANCE WHEN
YOU NEED IT**

HSOCIAL2018

THE WORLD IS BETTER
WITH
Romance

Harlequin has everything from contemporary, passionate and heartwarming to suspenseful and inspirational stories.

Whatever your mood,
we have a romance just for you!

Connect with us to find your next great read, special offers and more.

f /HarlequinBooks

🐦 @HarlequinBooks

www.HarlequinBlog.com

www.Harlequin.com/Newsletters

HARLEQUIN®

A *Romance* FOR EVERY MOOD™

www.Harlequin.com

Earn points on your purchase of new Harlequin
books from participating retailers.

Turn your points into **FREE BOOKS**
of your choice!

Join for FREE today at
www.HarlequinMyRewards.com.

Harlequin My Rewards is a free program (no fees)
without any commitments or obligations.

MYR18